Tiger Trap

Other Tiger Titles by Eric Walters

Tiger by the Tail
Tiger in Trouble
Tiger Town

Also by Eric Walters

Bifocal
Boot Camp
The Bully Boys
Caged Eagles
Camp 30
Camp X
Camp X: Fool's Gold
Death by Exposure
Diamonds in the Rough
Elixir
Grind
Hoop Crazy
House Party
The Hydrofoil Mystery
I've Got an Idea
Laggan Lard Butts
The Money Pit Mystery
Northern Exposures
Overdrive
Rebound
Run
Safe as Houses
Shattered
Stand Your Ground
Stars
Stuffed
Trapped in Ice
Triple Threat
Underdog
War of the Eagles
We All Fall Down

Tiger Trap

Eric Walters

A SANDCASTLE BOOK
A MEMBER OF THE DUNDURN GROUP
TORONTO

Editor: Michael Carroll
Designer: Erin Mallory
Printer: Webcom

Library and Archives Canada Cataloguing in Publication

Walters, Eric, 1957-
Tiger trap / Eric Walters.

ISBN 978-1-55002-673-3

I. Title.

PS8595.A598T588 2007 jC813'.54 C2007-900905

1 2 3 4 5 11 10 09 08 07

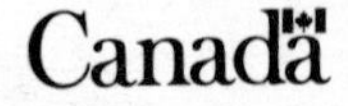

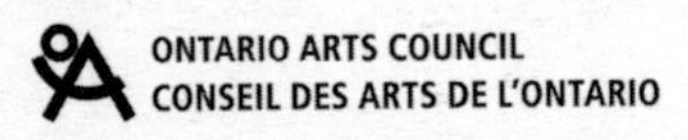

We acknowledge the support of the **Canada Council for the Arts** and the **Ontario Arts Council** for our publishing program. We also acknowledge the financial support of the **Government of Canada** through the **Book Publishing Industry Development Program** and **The Association for the Export of Canadian Books**, and the **Government of Ontario** through the **Ontario Book Publishers Tax Credit program** and the **Ontario Media Development Corporation**.

Care has been taken to trace the ownership of copyright material used in this book. The author and the publisher welcome any information enabling them to rectify any references or credits in subsequent editions.

J. Kirk Howard, President

Printed and bound in Canada
www.dundurn.com

Dundurn Press
3 Church Street, Suite 500
Toronto, Ontario, Canada
M5E 1M2

Gazelle Book Services Limited
White Cross Mills
High Town, Lancaster, England
LA1 4XS

Dundurn Press
2250 Military Road
Tonawanda, NY
U.S.A. 14150

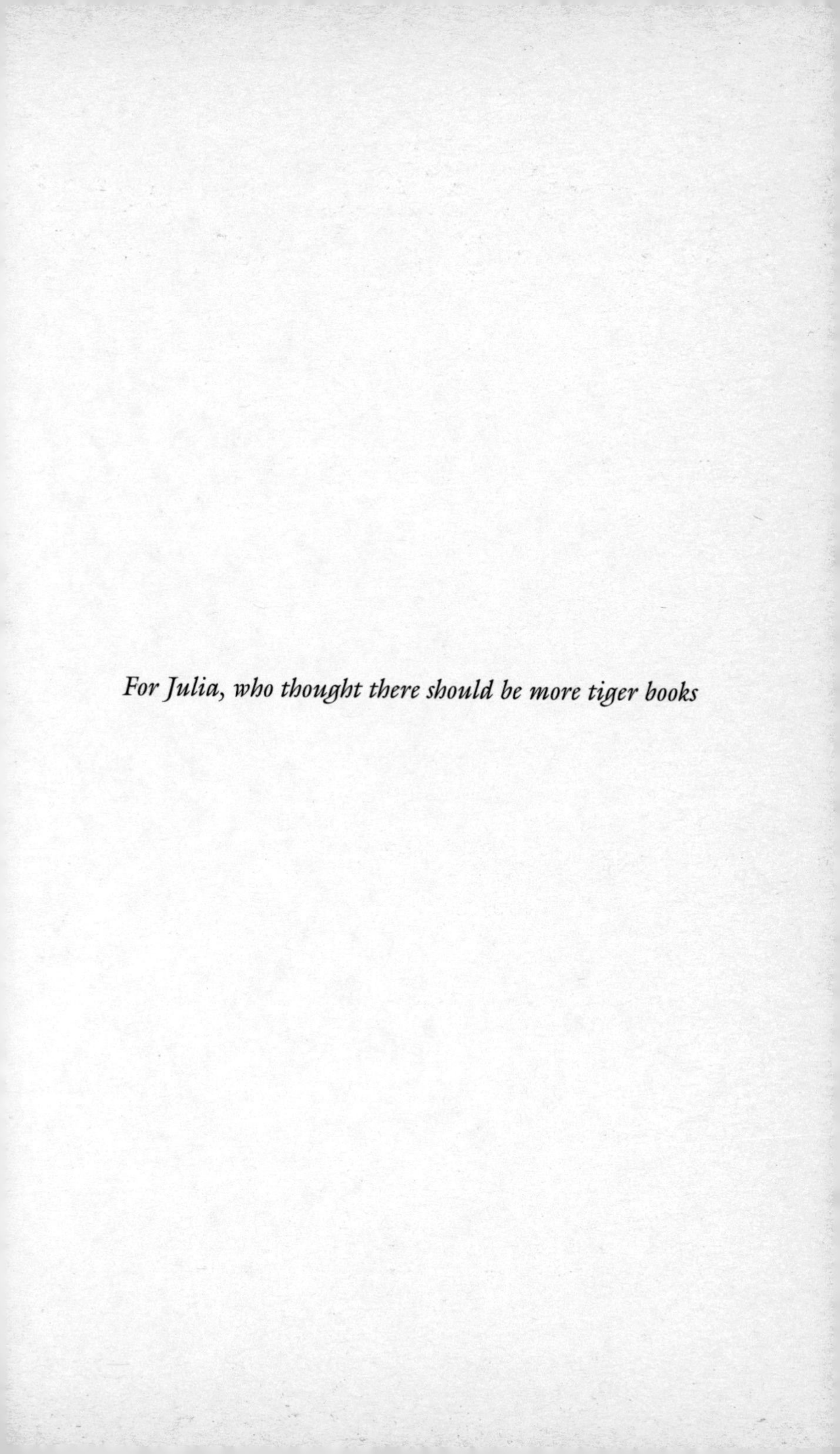

For Julia, who thought there should be more tiger books

Chapter 1

"Some people are just pigs," I said to myself as I reached down and picked up another ice-cream-bar wrapper from the ground. I dropped it into the garbage can that sat right beside where the wrapper had been dropped. It seemed like no matter how many garbage cans we placed around the property there were some people who just didn't care.

Although I guess I really shouldn't complain that much, because it was my idea to sell the ice-cream bars in the first place. And more people meant more ice-cream bars, which meant more money, and we needed money to feed the animals. Speaking of which, the animals weren't going to feed themselves.

I walked back over to the food cart, a three-wheeled contraption Mr. McCurdy had built. Awkward to push around, it was large enough to hold all the meat the big cats ate. It was truly amazing how much food they could go through. A full-grown male tiger could eat more than forty-five kilograms of meat in one meal, though we would never dream of feeding one that much at once.

Almost on cue there was a tremendous roar, and the hairs on the back of my neck stood on end. No matter how many times I heard Simba roar, it still had that effect on me. There was maybe nothing in nature as amazing — and as frightening — as the roar of a lion. He roared again.

"I'm coming!" I yelled. "Keep your mane on!"

I pushed the cart a little faster. I was slightly behind schedule, and the animals always seemed a little impatient, as if they knew the schedule and could also tell time to know I was late. More likely they probably just smelled me coming or, I guess, sniffed the food cart coming. There were a lot of dead chickens, not to mention pieces of deer, along with other assorted chunks of roadkill.

Simba roared for a third time, and I doubled my pace. Sometimes he got all the other cats going and then the wolves would join in. The visitors to the game farm loved the noise, but I knew it bothered the buffalo and the deer.

As I approached his pen, Simba came right up to the fence. His tail twitched angrily back and forth and his golden eyes glared intensely at me. Even through the fence — the safe, high, metal chain-link fence — I still felt my heart flutter and my stomach rise into my throat. I knew in the logical, thinking part of my brain that I was safe and that Simba couldn't possibly get out and grab me. But there was another part — the long-ago, under-evolved monkey part of the brain — that wanted me to run away and climb to the very top of the tallest tree I could find.

Really that made no sense. For one thing, not only couldn't I outrun a lion, but I never had been very good at climbing trees. Now my brother, Nicholas, he was a different matter. He could climb trees like nobody's business. Then again, he really hadn't evolved very far from the monkeys.

I lifted the cart's lid, and the smell of raw meat wafted up at me. Bending slightly away from the opening, I reached in and pulled out a chicken — a dead, headless, plucked chicken.

Simba raised a paw and pressed it against the fence, which gave ever so slightly against his force. I ducked under the handrail behind which visitors stayed and walked along the fence. Simba paralleled me on the other side of the fence. I moved until I came to the porthole — an opening in the fence large enough to put a chicken through. Simba put one of his front paws on the porthole, then reached out through it, demonstrating that the porthole was also big enough for a lion to get his *own* food if it came too close.

Suddenly, *I* felt like food, and stepped back to get safely out of the range of the roving paw. I waited for Simba to back off, but he didn't. With Simba perched right there, I had no way to get the chicken through the opening. If I tossed it toward the porthole, Simba could just grab it and pull it through. Or maybe he would knock it down and it would be there outside the cage on the ground and out of his reach. There was no way I was going to go and get it if that happened.

I looked up at the top of the fence. Would it be possible for me to toss the chicken that high? It was almost three metres tall and was topped by strands of barbed wire that extended above that. On the very top was a single strand of electric wire, just as there was with every cage holding a big cat. It held a current of electricity that wouldn't kill a cat but would certainly deliver enough of a sting to make it let go and drop back to the ground. I had obviously never climbed to the top and touched one of the wires, but I had accidentally backed into a similar wire we used to keep the deer in their pen. It had felt like a whole lot of bees buzzing around in my butt — an experience I hoped never to repeat.

The fence was pretty high, but I thought I could probably toss the bird over it. I grabbed the chicken by the neck and started to swing it back and forth, pumping my arm, and then at the highest point I let it fly. It flew into the air, higher and higher, hit the very top of the fence, the electric wire, and then began to tumble over and … stuck. The chicken got hung up on the very top of the fence!

Great, there was a dead chicken tangled up on the electric wire. How would I get it down? Would the wind just blow it off, or would it stay there and rot? And what about the electrical current in the wire? Would it slowly cook the chicken? Was that possible? Would it start to smell because it was rotten or because it was cooking?

Suddenly, Simba jumped into the air, threw his weight against the fence with a thunderous crash, and sent me backwards, almost tumbling over the handrail before I regained my balance. The big cat fell back to the ground, the fence rocked, and the chicken dropped off. Simba then sprang forward and scooped up the chicken in his mouth. The bird almost completely disappeared with a sickening crunch.

"That was quite the catch, Sarah."

I turned around. It was Nicholas, my eleven-year-old brother.

"Certainly a much better *catch* than the *throw* you made," he continued. "Though the best part was when you almost fell over the handrail. I thought your gracefulness was only surpassed by your throwing arm."

"Have you finished changing the water in all the pens?" I asked. I was trying to switch the subject because I knew it was hard to beat my brother in one of these arguments.

"I'm getting there."

"And what does that mean?"

"It means I've done a number of the pens."

"And would that number be sixteen or seventeen, like in all of them?"

"More like five, but five is still a number."

"Then maybe you should stop standing around annoying me and make that number bigger."

Nicolas saluted. "Yes, *sir*!"

"It's about time you showed me a little respect."

"I don't know what you mean, Sarah. I've always tried to give you as little respect as possible."

"You better get going before I toss a dead chicken at you."

"That's not a really dangerous threat. After all, I've seen you throw." He started snickering to himself.

I fought the urge to reach into the food cart, grab a chicken, and wing it at him. But what was the point? He was right. Even if I did throw it, I wouldn't hit him.

"Just get going ... okay?" My voice sounded more like a desperate plea than an order.

Nick strolled away, and I headed toward the next pen.

It was next door and held one of our newest animals.

"Hello, Woody," I said as I came up to the pen.

Woody trotted right up to the fence. While Simba was scary, Woody was just playful. Acting like a big brown house cat, he pressed his body against the fence and rubbed back and forth, rising on his back legs to put more pressure against the fence. I ducked under the handrail and put my hand against the fence so I could tickle Woody behind the ear. Normally, I wouldn't do this to a big cat, especially a big cat who was new and who I didn't know that well, but Woody was different.

He was a male lion, just like Simba, but he had been "fixed" when he was little. That meant he looked more like a female lion and would never grow as big or developed a mane as Simba. He also never roared. Instead he made a little meowing sound like a house cat. And I guess, really, he was a big house cat. Woody had been the mascot of a motorcycle gang and had lived in their clubhouse. He spent the first two years of his life wandering around eating pretzels and burgers and lapping up beer. Woody would have still been living with the bikers if the city hadn't changed the bylaws making it illegal to have a lion. That meant Woody either had to be put down or find another place to live. And that was why he had come to live at Mr. McCurdy's farm, which we had recently named Tiger Town.

Woody had only been here about a month, but the bikers had already visited him twice. They were big and bearded and dressed in leather when they roared up on their Harley-Davidsons. I had been next to Woody's pen that first time. We both heard the bikes. I didn't know what it was. He did. He got all frisky and excited.

I didn't know what those bikers did or didn't do, but judging from the way Woody acted when they appeared, they'd been good to him.

It was interesting watching all the other visitors to the farm watching the bikers. It was obvious that people were curious. And scared. Strange, but I didn't find them scary at all. Maybe it was because they treated Woody well, and I always thought that anybody who liked animals was okay. Maybe it was just because after spending all my time around lions and tigers I wasn't that scared of much of anything.

"I've got your breakfast, Woody," I said.

Woody sat on his back haunches as if he knew what I'd said and what was going to happen next. I dropped the chicken in through the porthole. Woody didn't move. He merely sat there, waiting. He was such a well-behaved lion — words that didn't normally go together too often.

"Okay, Woody, you can have it."

He got up and walked over to the chicken. Carefully, almost gently, he took it in his mouth. It looked as if he was trying to eat it without hurting it.

"Sorry I can't give you any pretzels to go along with the chicken."

"Excuse me."

I turned around. A woman and a girl — around my brother's age — stood behind me.

"I was wondering if I could ask you a question?" the woman asked.

"It's all part of the job." People were always asking questions. I hoped she wasn't going to ask me if I was serious about the pretzels.

"It's not really a question about the animals."

"That's okay. I can answer questions about anything here at Tiger Town." My mother always said there was no such thing as a stupid question. After fielding questions here, I knew she was wrong.

"Actually," the woman said, "my question is about your job. My daughter —" she gestured to the girl at her side "— loves animals. She wants to have a career working with them, but she doesn't realize you have to go to school for a long time and get a really good education before that can happen. We were wondering what sort of education she needs to get a job like yours."

I shook my head. "I really don't know."

"Well, what education do you have? Do you have a degree in zoology or biology, or are you a veterinarian?"

"I don't have any degrees … not yet, anyway. I'm in grade eight. I'm only fourteen."

"I … I'm sorry," the woman stammered. "I just thought you were older."

"That's okay," I said. People often did think I was older. Older, like fifteen or so, but not older like an adult. My brother always said it wasn't that I *looked* older but that I *acted* older. He said about fifty or sixty years old because I had stopped acting like his mother and had begun acting like his *grandmother*. He was lucky I wasn't his mother or grandmother, or he would be grounded until *he* was a grandfather.

"So this isn't a full-time job," the woman said.

"No, it's what I do on weekends and evenings. I'm a volunteer. We're all just volunteers."

"But there must be some experts who are in charge."

"There are," I agreed. "There's Mr. McCurdy and Vladimir. They're in charge."

"That's good to hear. Are *they* zoologists?"

"They're experts — real experts who know everything about animals. But they learned sort of on the job."

"What sort of job did they have?" she asked.

"They both worked for the circus."

"The circus! They must have *some* sort of formal education!"

"I don't really know about Vladimir," I said, though I was pretty sure he didn't. "But Mr. McCurdy dropped out of school long before he finished high school."

"It's hard to believe they'd put somebody in charge who doesn't even have a high-school diploma."

"Nobody *put* him in charge." Now I was starting to feel irritated. I knew she was trying to make some point to her daughter about an education, but it felt more like she was calling me a liar or disrespecting Mr. McCurdy. "Mr. McCurdy owns half the animals and Vladimir owns the other half."

"But where did they even get all these animals?"

"Some are from Mr. McCurdy's days in the circus. He brought them with him when he retired back to this farm. Others belonged to Vladimir. And all the latest animals were just sort of donated."

"Donated?"

I nodded. "Sometimes people have an animal they can't keep. They're looking for a new home for it."

"When you say 'people,' do you mean like people at another zoo?"

"Not zoos. People. People have an exotic animal they can't keep for one reason or another and they need to find a new home for it."

"I can see that with a cat or a dog," the woman said. "I just can't imagine that people have a tiger or lion they don't want. Actually, I can't imagine people even *having* a lion or a tiger."

I laughed. "A year ago I wouldn't have believed it myself. You'd be surprised. People have lions and tigers and bears that they keep in their barns and basements and garages."

"That's hard to believe."

"The proof is all around you," I said, gesturing at the pens that surrounded us.

"Amazing," she said, shaking her head slowly. "Just amazing."

"I've got to get back to work," I said. "Do you have any more questions I can answer?"

"Not really," the woman said.

"I have one," the daughter said.

I looked at her. "Go ahead."

"Do you think I could work here?"

I smiled. "Go up to the farmhouse and talk to Mr. McCurdy. Tell him I sent you."

"Thanks," she said.

Chapter 2

"Hello!" I yelled out as I entered the farmhouse. I didn't really need to knock before entering because Mr. McCurdy was almost like a grandfather to us, but I still always felt I should announce my entrance.

"Is anybody here?" I called.

"Go away, ugly girl!"

For a split second I was taken aback but, of course, I knew who it was.

"*You* go away!" I answered. I wanted to say more, but there was no point in arguing … with a parrot.

I walked into the kitchen. Mr. McCurdy was sitting in the corner, his ear glued to the telephone. He gave me a nod and a wave. Mr. McCurdy spent a lot of time on that phone, which was strange considering he didn't even have one — and claimed he didn't even *want* one — until my mother made him do it. She finally convinced him he couldn't run a business without having a phone. He'd argued he wasn't running a business; he was running a farm. But as more and more people wandered down the lane each day to see the animals, it became obvious who was right and he agreed.

Polly, the parrot, sat in the far corner on top of the kitchen cupboards. She had her head turned, one huge eye staring right at me. Polly didn't seem to like me very much. Actually, Polly didn't like *anybody* very much.

"Stupid, ugly girl," Polly muttered. "You *stink*. Take a bath!"

I fought the urge to say something back, but knew if I did get into an argument with a parrot I'd really be a stupid girl. Instead I reached over and opened one of the cupboards. There it was, what I was looking for, a box of crackers.

Polly straightened as she saw me grab the box. I opened it and slowly, deliberately, took out a cracker. Holding up the cracker, I turned it in my hand, looking at it from all angles, letting Polly have a good view of it. If she had been a dog instead of a parrot, she would have been drooling.

I glanced up at the bird. "Polly want a cracker?"

She twisted her head to peer at me with her other eye.

I held out my other arm, offering the parrot a perch. "Come on, Polly."

The bird opened her wings, and a rainbow of red, yellow, green, and blue feathers floated down. I tensed the muscles in my arm as she landed. She wasn't heavy, but I could feel the tips of her claws right through my jacket and shirt. I knew those claws were sharp enough to pierce my clothing and even the flesh of my arm.

"Polly want a cracker?" I asked again.

The parrot opened and closed her beak with a loud click. From what I'd been told that beak was powerful enough to snap a finger in two … and I was taunting her with a cracker. Not such a wise move, but it was what I had to do, what we all had to do if Polly was going to learn some manners.

I took a deep breath and felt Polly tighten her grip on my arm. "What do you have to say if you want the cracker?"

Polly fluffed out her feathers. It looked as if she had also taken a deep breath. "Please," she said.

"Good girl!"

I held out the cracker, and like lightning, she reached out and snatched it from my fingers — thank goodness, just grabbing the snack and leaving my fingers behind. Polly spun the cracker around in her mouth, snapped it into pieces, and swallowed it.

"What do you say now?" I asked.

"Thank you ... ugly girl."

Polly jumped off my arm and flew back to her perch atop the cupboards. I glanced down at my arm. There was a large white stain — bird crap!

"Oh, that's awful!"

Rushing over to the sink, I ripped off a piece of paper towel and wiped at the splotch. The only good thing was that my brother hadn't been here to witness Polly's accident. Although, to be honest, I didn't think it was an accident. That bird seemed to be pretty precise in just where and when she did that.

I walked back over, picked up the box of crackers, and took out two more. Waving them in the air to make sure Polly could see them, I popped them into my mouth. They were old and stale, but I didn't care. I smiled as I chewed and swallowed them.

"Greedy girl," Polly sputtered.

"Stupid, ugly bird," I replied. So much for teaching the bird manners.

I put the box of crackers back into the cupboard and closed the door tightly. If it was even slightly ajar, Polly could get in — she'd done it more than once. Despite what I'd said, that parrot was far from stupid.

Looking across the room, I spotted Laura. She was rolled up in a ball, her belly in the air, her long tail wrapped around her like a thin blanket. Laura's chest moved as she breathed, and I could hear her snoring ever so softly. I was so grateful for both the sight and the sound. Laura was almost fifteen years old — that was really, really old for a cheetah — and I knew she didn't have a long time left.

I made my way over and took up a spot on the couch beside her. Reaching down, I gave her a little rub behind the ears where I knew she loved to be stroked. Laura opened one eye and peered up at me. She pressed her head harder against my hand, closed her eyes again, and made that little growling sound that I knew was her way of purring. I kept rubbing her head.

"That's awful!" Mr. McCurdy said loudly into the phone.

I turned away from Laura. What was awful?

"People like that should be put in cages!" he thundered. "No, a cage is too good for 'em! They should be shot!"

Without hearing or knowing anything else, I knew this outburst had something to do with animals. For the most part that didn't take a genius to figure out because most of Mr. McCurdy's conversations involved animals.

"So how long are we talking about?" he asked. There

was an answer I couldn't hear. "That's not long, but if that's the way it is, that's the way it is. I'll be there tomorrow, and thanks for calling." He hung up the phone.

"Morning, Sarah," he said. "Do you know who I was just talking to?"

I shook my head. I knew what he was talking about, but not who he was talking to.

"That was the head of the humane society up near Woodstock. They were answering a complaint about a man with exotic animals."

I now also knew where this conversation was going.

"And they discovered that the animals were being badly treated, so they had to seize them and —"

"And they were wondering if you could take them and you said yes," I finished, cutting him off.

"Yeah … how did you know that?"

"It wasn't hard. What sort of animals are we talking about?"

"A lion, a leopard, a couple of half-wolf, half-dogs, and a pair of baby —"

"That's going to cost a lot of money," I objected.

"It won't cost us anything, Sarah. We're getting them for *free*."

"Maybe we're getting them free, but that doesn't mean keeping them will be free. First we have to build enclosures."

"We still have lots of materials left around, and Vladimir's a whiz when it comes to building."

"And then we have to feed them," I said. "It costs money to feed these animals."

"It's only a couple of more mouths to feed," Mr. McCurdy argued.

"Big mouths leading to big bellies."

"We're making good money with all these visitors and the things they buy at the concession stand and the donations. We're doing just fine."

"We're not doing that fine."

"Sarah, you worry too much."

"Somebody has to worry." I knew exactly how much money came in and how much was going out for expenses. Maybe nobody else cared to keep track of those things, but somebody had to. Perhaps people thought I was older than fourteen because I always had to act as if I were older. I understood my little brother acting like a kid because he was, but sometimes I thought Mr. McCurdy was ten instead of in his seventies.

"I'll take care of everything, so don't you worry," he said.

"It's just that we can't be taking in every animal that nobody wants."

"What choice do we have? If we don't take these animals, they're going to be put down."

"Put down?"

He nodded. "That's what the guy on the phone said. If we can't give 'em a home, they have no choice but to put them to sleep. So *I* don't have any choice."

It seemed as if everybody within hundreds of kilometres of here had heard about Tiger Town. That meant we weren't just getting visits but all sorts of calls asking to take animals that nobody else wanted.

"Trust me, Sarah," Mr. McCurdy said. "It'll be okay."

I did trust him. I just didn't trust him to think with his head instead of his heart. There was only so much anybody could do, only so much money or space to care for all these animals.

"Now I have to ask you a favour," he said.

"What sort of favour?"

"I have to leave right after we close up tonight and I have to take Vladimir with me and —"

"And you want to know if I can stay here overnight and watch the place," I said, completing his sentence.

"Yep. Nick can stay with you, and I'll leave Calvin to help out."

"Calvin's always a bundle of help," I said, referring to Mr. McCurdy's semi-trained chimpanzee.

"I can take him with me if you want," Mr. McCurdy said.

"Actually, it would probably be easier if you took Nick and left the ape."

Mr. McCurdy exploded in a burst of raspy laughter. "Then you'll stay?"

I nodded. "Of course I'll stay."

"That's my girl! We'll just close down the place tomorrow so there won't be any visitors."

"We can't do that. Sunday's our busiest day … the day we make the most money."

"I could maybe wait a day," he said.

"But then I couldn't help you. I have to be in school."

"I keep forgetting about that. I guess because when I was your age I'd already dropped out of school. I just wish we had another hired hand around here."

"So do I. But there's not enough money for that. You just go. I'll ask my mother and Martin to come over and help." Martin was my mother's boyfriend — did that ever sound strange — as well as the chief of police.

"You think they'd be willing to pitch in a hand?" Mr. McCurdy asked.

"I'm sure they will. Plus we have the other volunteers." Lots of local people came and offered to clean cages or prepare food for the animals or even sell treats at the concession stand. "We'll do fine."

Mr. McCurdy smiled. "With you in charge I know everything will be okay. I have complete confidence in you, Sarah."

I smiled back. I was glad he felt that way. I just wish I felt the same thing about myself.

Chapter 3

I heard the sound of a vehicle coming down the lane. Didn't these people know how to read signs? We'd been closed for almost an hour, and I wasn't letting anybody come in now no matter how much they begged or what excuse they made. The day had gone okay — stressful but okay. Even though my mother and Martin had been around, it still was me who was in charge. They were here to help, but I was the one responsible for keeping everything going.

The engine noise got louder, and then the vehicle appeared over the rise in the lane — it was Mr. McCurdy and Vladimir! They were back, and that meant I wasn't in charge anymore. I felt as if a great weight had been lifted off my shoulders.

The air brakes puffed and the gears ground together as the truck slowed down and came to a stop right in front of me. Vladimir practically jumped out of the cab and leaped to the ground.

"How big girl Sarah doing?" Vladimir asked in his heavy Russian accent.

He rushed over, picked me up off the ground, and planted a big kiss on one cheek and then the other. I'd almost gotten used to his Russian greetings, but even if I hadn't, what was I going to do? Vladimir was one colossal mountain of a man who towered over my head. Actually, he soared over the heads of most people. Combine his size with his long, out-of-control hair and big bushy black beard and he looked more like a wild animal than a wild-animal expert. But he was just as gentle as he was large. If I asked him not to greet me that way, he would have stopped. But I knew it would have hurt his feelings and I didn't want to do that. I also had to admit it was kind of neat. There was nobody else I knew who could spin me around like that. It reminded me of the way my father used to do that when I was little. That was a long time ago — a very long time ago.

I glanced over at the truck and watched as Mr. McCurdy started to climb down from the cab. Without a word or a look both Vladimir and I rushed around to his side of the truck. We took up positions beneath Mr. McCurdy — close enough to catch him if he fell but far away enough not to insult or hurt his pride if he didn't fall.

Carefully, he got down. He seemed so small against the massive machine. So little and so old. He was still pretty spry for somebody his age, but I'd noticed there were times when he moved a little slower or his hand shook or he fumbled for words. Mostly that was when he was tired.

"Did he sleep at all?" I whispered to Vladimir.

"Little, maybe few minutes," he answered quietly.

Finally, Mr. McCurdy reached the ground. "So how's my girl?" he asked, giving my hand a squeeze.

"I'm good. Everything's good."

"That's what I figured. I knew you could take care of everything. You always do me proud."

That made me feel good. I liked making Mr. McCurdy happy. I'd only known him a little longer than a year, but in that time he'd become so important to my family and I knew we were important to him. He was like a grandfather to me and Nick. Sometimes he was grouchy and grumbled about things, but I figured real grandfathers were like that some of the time, too.

"So there were no problems?" he asked.

"Nothing I couldn't handle." There had been a little boy tossing rocks at the deer, and I'd had to toss him out. The little boy should have been grateful that it was me that made him leave instead of Vladimir. Vladimir, as gentle as he was, got scary when somebody was mean to an animal. He wouldn't have just tossed the kid off the farm; he would have thrown him *through the air* and off the farm.

"So where's Nicky?" Mr. McCurdy asked.

"My mother took him home an hour or so ago. He had homework to do."

"And you didn't have any homework?"

"I did all mine Friday night."

"Where's Calvin?"

"Inside, watching TV."

Mr. McCurdy shook his head. "Worst mistake I ever made was letting you talk me into getting a television," he said to Vladimir.

"Vladimir like television."

"So does that blasted ape!" Mr. McCurdy snapped. "He just sits there all day in front of that set, drinking

Coke, holding that remote, flipping through the channels searching for a nature show."

I laughed.

"Glad you think it's funny! It's not so funny in the middle of the night when he's got the television on and the volume up. I think that ape is going deaf! Didn't he keep you awake last night?" Mr. McCurdy asked me.

"He did for a while, but then I turned the TV off."

"He let you do that?" Mr. McCurdy asked, surprised. "Didn't he just turn it back on?"

"He tried. I pulled the plug out of the wall when he wasn't looking. He couldn't figure out why it wouldn't turn back on. He just sat there, pushing the buttons on the remote. If it hadn't been so funny, I would have felt sorry for him."

"That's good to know," Mr. McCurdy said. "Maybe I can have a good sleep tonight. I could use one. I didn't sleep at all last night."

"Told Angus to sleep while driving back," Vladimir said.

"I couldn't sleep while you were driving," Mr. McCurdy said. "I had to keep my eyes on the road." He peered at Vladimir. "Who exactly taught you how to drive?"

"Nobody teach. Learn by self."

"That figures. I'm just surprised anybody ever gave you your licence."

"Licence? What mean licence?"

"You know, a piece of paper that says you can drive," Mr. McCurdy explained.

"I have licence. *Russian* driving licence."

"That figures. Didn't think you had one from this country."

"No need from this country. Vladimir Russian, so only need Russian licence. Besides, pay good money for licence. Give driving instructor lots of money, over five hundred rubles, to get licence."

"You mean you bribed him?"

"Of course bribe. Give bribe is Russian way of life and Vladimir Russian!" he almost shouted, pounding a fist against his chest.

Mr. McCurdy shook his head. "Enough of this. Let's have a look at these animals."

We circled around to the back of the big eighteen-wheeler. It belonged to a friend of Mr. McCurdy who let him borrow it whenever he needed it. Vladimir unhooked the door and pushed it up with a loud crash.

"Try and be a little more delicate, will you?" Mr. McCurdy said. "We're trying to keep the animals calm, not give 'em a heart attack."

Vladimir helped Mr. McCurdy and me up into the back of the truck, then climbed up after us. Mr. McCurdy hit a switch, and the entire back of the truck lit up in a fluorescent glow.

"Come and have a look," Mr. McCurdy said. "The lion's a full-grown female. Isn't she a beauty?"

The big tawny lion was in the first cage. She was long, but she looked thin, as if she hadn't been fed enough.

"Vladimir like leopard. Good leopard," he said, pointing to the spotted cat pacing around in the little cage across from the lion.

"What about the wolf-dogs?" I asked. I didn't see them.

"Shucks, they weren't wolves at all," Mr. McCurdy

said. "Looked to be some sort of husky-German shepherd cross. Not wolves at all. Left 'em with the humane society people."

"Oh," I said.

"You disappointed?" Mr. McCurdy asked.

"A little, I guess," I admitted. I should have been grateful. It meant fewer mouths to feed and less money needed to do the feeding.

"I thought you'd be happy about what we did bring," Mr. McCurdy said.

"The lion's okay … so is the leopard."

"But what about the babies?" he asked.

"Babies … there are babies?"

Mr. McCurdy turned to me. "I told you there were babies."

That was right. He had told me something — or tried to tell me something about babies, but I'd cut him off.

"What sort of babies?" I asked. I certainly didn't see any babies. I didn't see any animals except the lion and the leopard. Maybe they were lion cubs and were tucked away under their mommy, nursing or sleeping. Little lions were so cute.

"Two baby joeys," Mr. McCurdy said.

"You named them both Joey?" That sounded strange.

"I didn't *name* them Joey. They *are* joeys. That's what you call a baby kangaroo."

"We have kangaroos — baby kangaroos!" I cried, searching anxiously around the truck. I didn't see any kangaroos. The rest of the cages were empty — except for a large cardboard box sitting in the back corner of one of the cages. It was held in place with bungee cords attached to the bars. “Are they there?” I asked, my voice barely a whisper.

Mr. McCurdy nodded.

“Are they okay?”

Mr. McCurdy and Vladimir exchanged a worried look, but neither answered. Vladimir slipped the bolt on the door and swung it open. He bent down to get through the door and enter the cage. Carefully, slowly, almost delicately, he reached into the box. When he stood back up, he had a brown bundle of fur in his hands. It looked like a gigantic mouse. Its back legs kicked ever so slightly. At least I knew it was alive.

“It’s okay … right?” I asked.

“This one good. Here,” Vladimir said, handing me the little kangaroo.

I pulled it tightly against my chest, slipping a hand underneath to support its legs. It stopped kicking and snuggled against me. It was soft and warm.

“Second one good, too,” Vladimir said. He had the other one in his arms. It was probably the same size but seemed smaller against him.

“They’re so tiny,” I said.

“Just babies,” Mr. McCurdy said. “Way too young to be away from their mama.”

“Then why are they away from her?” I asked.

“No choice.”

“You could have brought her along. We still have plenty of space. She could have lived right —” I stopped myself and got a sick feeling in my stomach. I already knew why she wasn’t here.

“Poor old girl,” Mr. McCurdy said. “Too old to have twins … wasn’t getting fed proper herself … no medical care ... filthy pens."

"Disgusting!" Vladimir said. "Disgusting how animals lived!"

"You saw where they kept the animals?" I asked.

"Just pictures," Mr. McCurdy said. "The pictures they took for evidence for the court proceedings against the owner."

"Thank goodness they got there in time to save the rest of the animals," I said.

Mr. McCurdy's face darkened. "They saved some of the animals."

"Some?" I asked, though I knew what he meant.

"So many of the animals were in such bad shape that there was nothing they could do. Better to put 'em down than let 'em suffer."

"That's so sad," I said.

"Vladimir wish he get hands on man who own animals. Vladimir make sure he never hurt anything again!" His eyes flashed angrily.

"At least they caught him and he'll get punished," I said, trying to deflect some of his anger.

"They caught him, but that doesn't mean he'll get much punishment," Mr. McCurdy said. "Probably get nothing more than a fine or a slap on the wrist."

"Vladimir give more than slap on wrist. Vladimir break skull or snap spine like twig."

I knew how gentle Vladimir was, but I could see him doing that to somebody who hurt an animal. "I guess we should just be grateful that these four animals are alive and well and survived."

"I hope they'll all survive, Sarah," Mr. McCurdy said.

I didn't like the sound of that.

"Don't get me wrong, Sarah. We're going to try our best, but I don't know much about kangaroos."

"Me, neither," Vladimir said. "Never care for kangaroo."

"But what I do know," Mr. McCurdy said, "is that these two are way too young to be away from their mother, and it's going to be hard work to try to raise 'em."

I glanced down at the little bundle pressed against my chest. At that same time it peered up at me with soft, gentle, liquid, expressive eyes. The joey seemed to be trying to tell me something. It opened its mouth, and a little pink tongue flicked up and touched my face. The tongue was rough and dry. I knew what it was trying to say now — it was hungry.

"I think the first thing we have to do is feed 'em," Mr. McCurdy said.

"What do kangaroos eat?" I asked.

"Kangaroos are grazers, like cows or deer. But baby kangaroos eat the same as every other baby mammal — milk."

"You mean we have to bottle-feed them?" I asked.

"Just like with the deer you helped raise," Mr. McCurdy said.

I'd helped bring up two little baby deer whose mother had died giving birth to them. They'd become my little girls, and they treated me like their mommy. They now lived out in the pen with all the other deer, eating grass and hay. They didn't need me anymore. Of course, that didn't stop them from coming right up to me when I came to their pen. They always pushed their little faces against the fence and suckled on my fingers.

"You really did such a good job on those deer," Mr. McCurdy said.

"Little deer die without big girl Sarah," Vladimir said. "Maybe Sarah keep baby roos alive, too."

"I'll do my best to help," I said.

"Me and Vladimir were hoping you could help a lot," Mr. McCurdy said. "Maybe starting tonight."

"Tonight?"

"We're both pretty beat, what with being up all night and the drive and everything, and they're going to need two, maybe three feedings through the night."

"But I have school tomorrow."

"Shoot, that's right!" Mr. McCurdy said. "I guess you can't help, so that means I'll have to do it."

"No!" I cried. He couldn't stay up another night. "I can do it."

"But what about school?"

"I'll go to sleep. I'll get up a few times to feed them and I'll sleep the rest of the night. It'll be fine. Honest."

"Are you sure?"

"Positive. I can do it. I'll feed them and fall right back to sleep again. No problem."

"That's great, Sarah. We'll make up a big batch of kangaroo formula."

"You have a formula for kangaroos?" I asked.

"Vladimir have recipe for all animals. Fix big batch. Put in bottles."

"That would be great," I said. "Then if you could just drive me and the kangaroos to my house."

"Wouldn't it be easier to stay here?" Mr. McCurdy asked.

"Maybe easier, but if I want to sleep, I'm better off

in my room and in my bed."

"Is your mother going to be okay about you bringing home a couple of kangaroos?" Mr. McCurdy asked.

I actually hadn't thought of that. "I guess she will."

"Are you sure?"

"Positive." A smile came to my face. "After all, she's never, ever said anything to me about *not* bringing home kangaroos."

Both Vladimir and Mr. McCurdy burst into laughter. "That sounds like something your brother would say," Mr. McCurdy said.

"Hey! There's no need to insult me."

Chapter 4

"Sarah ... Sarah, it's time to get up," my mother called. "If you don't get up, you'll be late."

I opened one eye. It still wasn't even light, so how late could I be?

"Come on, Sarah, get up and I'll ... *aaahhhh!*"

As soon as my mother screamed, I sat bolt upright and watched as she jumped into the air and thumped down onto my bed, her knee in my stomach, flattening me into the mattress, knocking the wind out of me.

"Rats! Giant rats!" she yelled.

It was the kangaroos! She was seeing the joeys! In the dim light she couldn't see what they were — not that I could ever expect her to think there were kangaroos in my bedroom. She had been asleep when I brought them home in the night. I wanted to cry out and tell her, explain, but there wasn't enough air in my lungs.

"Kangaroo," I finally hissed.

"They're jumping up!" she howled. "They're trying to get us!"

The two little joeys were just doing what they'd

been doing almost all night — jumping up to get my attention.

My mother started shrieking louder and kicking her feet. If she hit one of the joeys, she could kill it! I didn't have much lung power, but I still had movement. I reached up, grabbed my mother, flipped her over, spun around, and pinned her to the bed, me on top now.

"Sarah, what are you doing?" she screeched.

"Don't hurt them," I said, forcing the words out. "Not rats … kangaroos … they're … kangaroos."

Even in the limited light, I could see her face twist into a mask of confusion.

"Kangaroos," I said again.

"But how did you —"

"Mom! Sarah! What's happening?" Nick cried out as he ran into the room. Before I could answer or react, he slid out of sight, thumping noisily to the floor.

I leaped off my mother and the bed. "Nick, are you okay?"

He sat up. "I'm fine … I slipped. Why were you both yelling?"

In answer the two little kangaroos bounced over to my side and began bumping into me, trying to force me to ignore my brother and notice them so I could feed them again.

"We have kangaroos!" Nick shouted. "Kangaroos!"

Suddenly, the room became bright. My mother had turned on a light. Both joeys bounded up and bounced off my legs. Even though my mother now knew they weren't giant rats, she still appeared anxious and upset.

"Sarah, why are there kangaroos in your room?" she asked.

"I figured it would be better to have them in here instead of your room," I said.

My mother's expression changed from anxious to annoyed, and Nick giggled.

"What are they doing *anywhere* in the house?" she asked. "And why didn't you ask permission to bring them here?"

"You were already asleep by the time I got home, and I didn't want to wake you up," I said. That was true. I'd deliberately waited until I was certain it was late enough to ensure she was asleep. "Besides, I didn't think you'd object."

"I probably wouldn't have objected, but you need to ask me. Besides, why did you need to bring them here instead of leaving them at Mr. McCurdy's? They're his, right?"

"No, Mom. I found them when I was walking home."

My mother gave me a warning glance. I think I'd been hanging around my brother too much, because that sounded like something he would have said, too.

"Mr. McCurdy and Vladimir brought them home last night," I said. "They rescued them. They're red kangaroos."

"They look brown to me," Nick said.

"They are brown, but as they get older, they'll develop a reddish tinge to their coats — especially the males. These are just joeys."

"Joeys? You named them both Joey?" Nick said, saying almost the same words I'd used myself.

"Don't be ridiculous!" I snapped. "Baby kangaroos are called joeys. I thought *everybody* knew that." There was no way I was going to admit I didn't know that myself until yesterday. Part of the job of being a big sister was knowing things that your little brother didn't know. The other part of the job was letting him *know* you knew things he didn't and acting superior.

"Okay, Sarah, let's hear it," Nick said.

"Hear what?"

"Hear everything you know about kangaroos that I don't."

Apparently, Nick *did* know my job, too.

"Well?" Nick prodded.

"What would you like to know?" I'd spent some time, between feedings, surfing the Net to find out more kangaroo facts and information.

"Just the *Reader's Digest* version, big stuff, important and interesting stuff."

"Okay. Kangaroos are from Australia."

"Even I know that," Nick said.

"They're marsupials, which means the females have pouches and they carry their young in those pouches."

"Gee, I know that, too," Nick said. "Maybe you don't know anything about them that I don't know."

Okay, if he wanted to be that way. "And I guess, of course, you know how many species of kangaroo there are, right?"

"A bunch," Nick said.

"Forty-seven is the correct number, ranging in size from the smallest, the rock wallaby, up to the largest, the red kangaroo, which stands as tall as 1.8 metres and can weigh up to 140 kilograms."

"Wow, that's big! I'd hate to meet up with a herd of them."

"A herd? What do you think they are — cows?"

"I don't know what you call a lot of kangaroos," Nick said.

"I do," I said smugly. "You call them a mob, and they can be large. It would be impressive to see them travelling. They can go as fast as seventy kilometres an hour. The big males can cover up to nine metres in one bound."

Nick whistled. "These guys will be able to jump that far someday?"

"Someday. The red kangaroo, or as it's called in Latin, the *Macropus rufus*, is an impressive animal." I didn't know if I'd said that correctly, but Nick wouldn't know if I made up words and said them in *pig* Latin. "*Rufus*, of course, means red, and *macro* refers to the largest. A female kangaroo is called a doe, flyer, roo, or jill, and the male is called a buck, boomer, or jock. And, of course, the baby, as *everybody* knows now, is called a joey.

"So if they're not called Joey, what are their names?" Nick asked.

"Officially, they don't have names, but I sort of named them. This one," I said, pointing at the slightly bigger of the two, "is Kanga. And the other one is called —"

"Roo!" both my mother and brother said in unison.

"Yeah. The kangaroos from *Winnie the Pooh* are the only ones I know."

"They're not very big," my mother said. "How old are they?"

"It's hard to say, maybe four months. Do either of you know how big a kangaroo is at birth?"

"No, but I'm sure you'll tell us," Nick said.

"Do you want to hear or don't you?" I asked.

He nodded.

"When they're first born, they're as small as this," I said, holding my fingers about two centimetres apart.

"Come on, no way," Nick said.

"It's true. They crawl up through their mother's fur and climb into her pouch. They stay in there, nursing, growing, until they become big enough to peek out. Altogether a joey is about eight months old before he completely abandons his mother's pouch."

"So these two should still be with their mother," my mother said.

"They should be. They would be … if she were still alive."

"What happened to her?" Nick asked.

"I don't know exactly. I just know the place they were keeping them wasn't very good. You know how bad some of these places can be."

"So rightfully," my mother said, "these two little babies should still be with their mother, nursing and sleeping in her pouch."

"They should be. That's why I had to bring them home. They have to be fed every few hours."

"All night?" Nick asked.

"All the time," I said.

"You were up all night feeding them?" my mother asked.

"Not all night," I said. "I got some sleep." Not much more than a few minutes at a time, I thought, but I had gotten some sleep. "They probably want to eat again."

"Can I help?" Nick asked.

"I don't know."

"Please?"

"Well … I guess you can," I said. I was actually

going to ask him to help, because two kangaroos really required two sets of hands, but this way was even better — now he thought I was doing him a favour instead of it being the other way around.

"Thanks!" he cried.

"There are a couple of bottles over on the dresser," I said.

Nick stood, took a step, then stopped. He lifted his foot and looked at the bottom. "What's that?" he asked, pointing at a dark smear on the bottom of his foot.

I knew exactly what it was.

He touched it with his hand. "*Uggg* ... it's ... it's —"

"Kangaroo poo," I said.

"That's awful! That's disgusting!" Nick squealed as he hopped around the room on one foot.

"It's not awful. It's fantastic!" I said.

"How can me stepping in poo be fantastic?" Nick demanded.

"Because you can't poo unless you eat, so I know that at least one of them is getting enough milk," I explained. "It's hard to know for sure if they're getting enough to eat because so much gets spilled or smeared on their fur, the floor, or my clothes."

"I'm glad you're happy, but that doesn't change the fact that this is disgusting!" Nick wailed.

"Don't be such a big baby. Go and wash off your foot and come back. And if you're not back soon, I'm not going to let you help."

"Okay, okay," Nick said, hopping out of the room.

"You better hurry up and feed them or we'll be late," my mother said. "I assume we have to deliver them to Mr. McCurdy's on our way to drop you two off at school."

"Actually," I said, pausing and taking a deep breath, "I was hoping you could drop me off at Mr. McCurdy's place, too."

"You mean instead of going to school?"

I nodded. "I haven't been away all year, and it's not like I can't afford to miss a day or two."

"Two?"

"I meant later on, if I was sick or something, not that I'm not going to go to school tomorrow. Well ...?"

"I guess a day would be okay."

"Thanks, Mom. I really appreciate it."

"Besides, it sounds like you were already doing a lot of work learning about kangaroos. Where did you learn all of those things?"

"Some I knew already. I did some surfing last night," I said, gesturing at the computer on the desk in the corner of my room. Actually, I didn't have much choice. One of the other things I'd learned about kangaroos — after they kept me up most of the night — was that they were nocturnal. They stayed awake at night.

"Now you better get moving," my mother said. "I still have to get out of here on time to get to work and get your brother to school, so if you want a ride you better hurry."

"I'll hurry ... and thanks."

Chapter 5

"Good afternoon, Sarah," Mr. McCurdy said. "Did you have a nice little nap?"

"It was good, but I don't think it was that little." I'd slept for close to two hours. "I guess I was more tired than I thought."

"Nap good. Still look tired," Vladimir said. "Go back to sleep if wish."

"I'm fine," I said.

I probably would still be sleeping if one of the roos hadn't tried suckling my nose. It was a rude awakening — my eyes had popped open and I'd found myself eyeball to eyeball with a kangaroo. I now understood why my mother had thought they were rats. For a split second when I opened my eyes I'd thought my nose was being gnawed by a gigantic mouse.

After I removed my nose from its mouth, I'd gotten up, given them both another bottle, and then gone looking for Mr. McCurdy and Vladimir. I'd finally found them huddled behind a small storage shed.

"So did you finish the pens for the new cats?" I asked.

"Put lion in with other female lion," Vladimir said. "Leopard in new pen. Finished, all fixed up good."

"Do you want me to help clean the pens?" I asked.

"Maybe later," Mr. McCurdy said. "Right now we have other things to take care of. We're doing some observing."

"What are we observing?" I asked.

"That man right there."

"Right where?" I asked.

Mr. McCurdy motioned with his head. "Around the other side of the shed."

I took a couple of steps so I could see around the side.

"Don't let him spot you!" Mr. McCurdy hissed, jumping back out of sight.

"Why not?"

"Because we don't want him to know we're watching him."

"But *why* are we looking at him?" I asked.

"Because I just got a bad feeling about him," Mr. McCurdy said. "A real bad feeling."

"Who is he?"

"Don't know. Came early this morning, knocked on the door, asked to see the animals, gave a donation, and has been here ever since. He's been here almost six hours."

"Maybe he just loves animals," I suggested. The weekends were the busy times for visitors, but it wasn't unusual for people to drop in during the week — there weren't as many, but sometimes they were the real serious animal watchers.

"Don't know about that," Mr. McCurdy said, "but he really does like that notebook of his. Do you see him making notes?"

I hadn't seen anything in the few seconds I'd been observing. "I guess he just wants to remember what he sees."

"Doubt it," Mr. McCurdy said. "I'd love to see what he's writing."

"Angus want see book, then Vladimir get book."

"How would you do that?" I asked.

Vladimir shrugged. "Easy. Vladimir go and take notebook from him."

"You can't do that!" I protested.

Vladimir laughed. "Course can do. Vladimir *big*. Just take notebook from him."

"You can't go around taking things from people," I said. "That sort of thing can get somebody arrested."

"Maybe somebody, but not Vladimir. Chief of police is Martin, and Martin Vladimir's friend. Friend not arrest Vladimir."

"It doesn't work that way," I said.

"Work that way in Russia."

"Yeah, but in Russia you bribe people to get your licence," Mr. McCurdy said. "Here, you hit somebody you could get arrested, even if the chief of police is your brother."

I knew that Martin would help Vladimir or Mr. McCurdy deal with any troubles that came up. In fact, without Martin's help, Mr. McCurdy's farm would have been closed instead of turned into an exotic animal park. He'd made sure they met all the bylaws and regulations, helped build the pens, figured out how to get grain and hay for the grazers, and arranged for the highway department to bring the roadkill over for the cats. He'd also, along with my mother's help as a lawyer, made arrangements so that Vladimir was now allowed to stay in the country.

Originally, Vladimir had come from Russia as a visitor on a two-week holiday. Instead of leaving at the end of his trip, he just sort of disappeared. How something as big as Vladimir could disappear was hard to imagine, but he'd managed to stay out of sight for two years. But now, with his new status, he didn't need to hide — he was legal.

"Let Vladimir go talk to man. Just ask for notebook. Be polite."

"I think it would be better if you stayed away from him, Vladimir," Mr. McCurdy said.

"I agree," I said.

"That's good," Mr. McCurdy said, "because I think *you* should go and talk to him."

"Me?" I gasped. "You want me to go down and take the notebook away from him?"

"Of course not," Mr. McCurdy said. "Just go down and talk to him. You can attract more flies with honey than you can with vinegar."

"Flies?" Vladimir said. "Why need more flies. Lots of flies on farm already."

"No, I don't want to attract flies," Mr. McCurdy said. "It's an old saying."

"Never understand old sayings of Angus," Vladimir said, shaking his head. "Never make sense. Words never mean what supposed to mean."

"It means that sometimes it's easier to get what you want if you're sweet instead of bitter," Mr. McCurdy said patiently. "Understand?"

"Understand some. Why we want attract flies?"

"We don't want to get more flies!" Mr. McCurdy said, now frustrated and annoyed. "Sarah, can you just go up and talk to him? He doesn't even know who you are. He knows Vladimir and me work here, but he hasn't seen you. Make like you're just another visitor here to see the animals."

"You want me to lie?" I asked.

"No, of course not! I just want you not to tell the truth."

"Now you're sounding like my brother."

"Shame Nick isn't here or I could ask him to go. That boy has a real creative way around the truth."

That was the most polite way I'd ever heard Nick described. He really didn't lie, but he had an interesting way of stretching and massaging the truth until it became a story that was more a work of fiction than fact. I thought he had a serious career in the future as a writer, or a used-car salesman. Or maybe a politician.

"What would I say to that man?" I asked.

"Start with hello and go from there," Mr. McCurdy said. "Or would you rather I send Vladimir here." He gestured to his large friend.

"No, I'll go," I said. "I don't want to, but I will."

"We'll wait for you here behind the shed," Mr. McCurdy said. "We'll watch and come quick if there's any problem. Go."

I took a deep breath, then stepped out from behind the shed. As I ambled along the path toward the man, I looked back over my shoulder. Vladimir was peeking out from the shed. He gave a little wave, then disappeared. I turned my attention to the pens I was passing, trying to appear casual, as if I was interested in the animals and not even noticing the man — the man who seemed like the only visitor to the park. Suddenly, he glanced up and looked right at me. I spun around so I was now peering directly into the pen in front of me — Buddha's pen. The big tiger sat at the back, holding a dead chicken between his massive front paws. Using his mouth, he was plucking it — pulling out the feathers and then spitting them out. The chicken was almost completely de-feathered. Buddha had this thing about feathers. Some big cats would just eat a chicken, feathers and all, while with others we pulled out the feathers before throwing the bird into their pens. Buddha liked to do it himself, though.

Out of the corner of my eye I saw the man still standing in front of the next cage. He was making notes again. If I was standing behind him right now, I could see what he was writing. Slowly, sidestepping, I slid over toward the next pen. I had this strange thought that if I didn't look at him, he couldn't see me creeping up on him. I stopped when I was standing in front of one end of the same pen as the man. What did I do now? I turned my head ever so slightly so I could see him. Head down, he was taking more notes.

I cleared my throat. "Nice tiger."

He glanced up. "What?"

"Nice tiger."

He shrugged.

"I like tigers," I said. "Do you like tigers?"

"Sure," he said, going back to his notes.

Okay, that wasn't working. "I know a lot about this tiger," I said. "Would you like to know about it?"

"I think I already know about it. Siberian tiger,

male, somewhere around fifteen years of age —"

"Seventeen years old," I said. Maybe I should be more direct.

He nodded. "Seventeen years old. The coat's nice. It looks like it's been receiving adequate care."

"Adequate?" I questioned. "He's been getting *great* care. All the animals are receiving great care!"

The man stared at me. He didn't seem angry, but he did have an intense expression, as if he were now studying me, as if I were one of the animals, as if he were going to make some notes in his book about me, as if he were trying to judge if I was receiving adequate care.

Was that what all those notes were about? Was he inspecting the animals because he worked for some agency that was checking to see if the animals were up to standards? Was this one more attempt to close down Tiger Town?

"You know this place meets everybody's standards, that all the animals and all the pens have been approved," I said.

"I'm not an inspector, but it sounds like you work here."

"No," I said nervously. Technically, I didn't *work* here — I *volunteered* here. "I just come here a lot and I know about the animals." There, that wasn't a lie.

"Do you know *everything* about the animals?"

There was a tone in his voice and a smirk on his face that suggested the question was more of an accusation. He was staring at me again. No, he wasn't looking *at* me as much as he was looking right *through* me, and I was sure he could tell what I was thinking and knew I'd been feeding him a lot of half-truths.

Funny, that was the same expression Martin had sometimes. The same look lots of policemen had. Wait a second. This guy had short hair and thick-soled black shoes, and he was big and muscular. Maybe he *was* a cop.

"Do you know how much this tiger is worth?" he said suddenly, motioning to the animal.

"What?" I asked. I understood the question but didn't know what he meant by it.

"Do you know how much a tiger is worth?"

"It depends," I answered warily.

He smirked again. "I guess it does. A baby tiger is worth at least five thousand dollars because people can put them in petting zoos and bring them to events, let people have their picture taken with it. A full-grown tiger, especially an old one like this, is practically worthless."

"Not necessarily," I said. "It could be worth a lot of money."

The man stopped smirking. "It could be, but only if it stops being an old tiger and becomes a *dead* tiger."

He studied me long and hard. Again I felt as if he could see right through me. I lowered my eyes to the ground.

"But the real question is, how would you know about that?" he asked.

"Well … I guess I don't. Not really."

"I see. Could I ask you a question?"

"Sure … I guess," I stammered.

"Do animals come and go from here?"

"Come and go?" What did he mean by that? Buddha had escaped once — practically the first time I'd met Mr. McCurdy last summer — and we'd recaptured him, but that was the only time. That is, if you didn't count the buffalo getting loose on the road. Or the time Peanuts, the elephant, wandered into the neighbour's cornfield. It was amazing how much corn and cornstalks an elephant could eat. But why did he want to know this? Was he a reporter? I hated reporters.

"Well?" he pressed. "Do animals disappear from here?"

"Never," I said. "They come — there's always new animals — but they never go."

"So you don't think they'd sell me this tiger?"

"You want to buy this tiger?" I got a terrible feeling in the pit of my stomach. Now I knew who this guy was. He was one of those awful people who buy and sell exotic animals. He wanted this tiger so he could kill it and sell off the body parts! "They don't sell animals here," I said curtly.

"Are you sure? Maybe if I offered them enough money, they'd sell it. Why don't you bring me over to meet the owners."

"Me?"

"Sure. Isn't that them over there, hiding behind that shed?"

I turned around in time to see Vladimir and Mr. McCurdy peek out from behind the shed, then disappear from sight when they realized we were watching them.

"That is them, isn't it?" he asked.

"Maybe. I really didn't see who it was."

"You didn't? That's strange. I could've sworn you were standing there behind that shed with them before you came over to talk to me."

That sinking feeling in my stomach became a gaping

pit. I didn't know what to say, what to do. I just wanted to run away.

"I'm going over to talk to them, so you might as well come along," he said.

He started walking toward the shed. That really wasn't a good idea. Once Vladimir found out the man was trying to buy tigers he'd pick him up and throw him off the property … say, that didn't seem like such a bad idea. I scrambled to catch up to the stranger.

"Hello," he called out as he reached the shed. Mr. McCurdy and Vladimir stepped out into the open. "Which of you two is in charge of this place?"

"Who's asking?" Mr. McCurdy asked.

"Who's asking isn't as important as why I'm asking."

"What's that supposed to mean?" Mr. McCurdy demanded.

"It means I have a business deal to discuss and I need to discuss it with the person who can do that business."

"What sort of business?" Mr. McCurdy asked.

"Are you the person in charge of this place?"

"I'm one of them," Mr. McCurdy said. "And this here's the second." He gestured to Vladimir. "We own and run the place."

"Excellent. Perhaps we could go and talk some business."

"Whatever you have to say you can say right here," Mr. McCurdy said.

The man looked at me, then back at Mr. McCurdy. "I really think this should be a private conversation."

"Whatever you have to say you can say in front of Sarah. She's an important part of this place. When we go away, she runs everything."

He turned back to face me. "I thought you didn't work here."

"Well ..."

"I knew you weren't telling the truth. You're not very good at lying."

"Never was very good," Mr. McCurdy agreed. "But you can still say what you want in front of Sarah."

"No, I can't," the man said, shaking his head. "I need to talk to you in private. Nobody but me and the two of you can be part of the conversation."

"And if we don't agree to that?" Mr. McCurdy asked.

"Then we don't talk and you won't know what it was I wanted to talk to you about."

"I guess I'll take that chance," Mr. McCurdy said. "You should leave now."

"Leave?"

"Yeah. Go. Get. Vamoose. Vanish. Disappear. Understand?"

"You're kicking me out?"

"No, I'm asking you to leave. If you don't leave, then I'll kick you out. Or, I guess, have my good friend, Vladimir, kick you out."

"Vladimir kick you off good," Vladimir said, stepping toward the man in a very threatening manner.

I involuntarily stepped back myself, but the man didn't budge.

"Listen to what I have to say and then, if you want, I'll leave. Nobody will have to kick me out."

Vladimir balled his hands into fists and stepped even closer. "Maybe Vladimir enjoy kicking man out."

"Look," I said as I moved forward and put myself

between Vladimir and the stranger, "I have to go, anyway. It's time for me to feed the kangaroos again and then I have to get home. So I'll leave and you three can talk."

"You don't have to go, Sarah," Mr. McCurdy said. "It's my farm and I decide who stays and who goes — not him."

"But I *want* to go," I said. "I *have* to go."

Mr. McCurdy didn't answer right away. That was good. It meant he was thinking it over. "Okay, we'll talk to this guy, just the two of us, but we're only doing it because Sarah wants us to. Not because anybody else does."

"I don't care why, as long as we do talk privately," the stranger said.

"Okay, I'm going," I said. "If I don't see you before I go home, I'll be back tomorrow. Is that okay? You two will take care of Kanga and Roo tonight?"

"All taken care of, Sarah," Vladimir said, turning to face the man. "Everything taken care of good ... *real* good."

A shudder went up my spine. I knew what Vladimir meant. It was better I was leaving. I didn't want to see what was going to happen next because it wasn't going to be pretty.

Chapter 6

"Sarah?"

Startled out of my thoughts, I glanced at my mother beside me at the kitchen table.

"Could you please pass Martin the potatoes?" she asked.

"Yeah, sure, of course." I picked up the serving bowl and passed it to my brother, who handed it to Martin.

The police chief had dinner at our house a couple of times a week. He and my mother seemed to be getting pretty serious. Maybe I should have been unhappy about my mother having a boyfriend, but he was nice and he did make her happy. A lot happier than my father had made her the last couple of years of their marriage. I wondered if my father was happy now — we didn't see him enough for me to know. Somehow I doubted it.

"So," Martin said, "your mother was telling me about the kangaroos."

"They're really cute. I named them Kanga and Roo," I said.

"That's cute, too. How are they doing?"

"Really good. They're eating well."

"And often," my mother said. "Sarah was up all last night feeding them."

"That's rough. Now that I'm chief I don't work the graveyard very often, but I remember those night shifts. You're so tired it feels like you can't even keep your eyes open."

"That's how you probably feel right now, Sarah," my mother said.

"I feel fine."

"Don't be silly," she said. "You must be tired. If I'd been up all night, I'd be —"

"But it wasn't you who was up," I snapped. "It was me! Just because *you* feel cold doesn't mean *I* need a sweater."

My mother seemed hurt by my comments, and I suddenly felt bad. I didn't mean to upset her, but it was happening a lot lately. Words just popped out of my mouth as if I were hearing them for the first time myself and were shocked by what I'd said.

"You look pretty tired to me, as well," Nick said.

I shot him a dirty look. He could be such a little suck-up sometimes — as if he'd never done anything to anger or offend Mom.

"I thought you were going to fall face first into your mashed potatoes," he continued. "You just drifted off a couple of times."

"That's not because I'm sleepy, but because I was lost in thought. Something you have very little experience with."

There was silence. Now if I could just think of something nasty to say to Martin I could have everybody at the table annoyed at me.

"It's been a week or so since I've been out to Tiger Town," Martin finally said. "How are Angus and Vladimir doing?"

"They're doing great," I said. "Everything's great … well, good … well, okay."

"Just okay?" he asked.

"Well … everything's good with the animals, and that's the most important part."

"Then what part is going just okay?" Martin pressed.

"I guess it's mainly the money," I admitted, feeling as if I didn't have the right to discuss Mr. McCurdy's finances, though I knew them better than anybody, including Mr. McCurdy.

"I thought that from the number of visitors I see at the park there would be enough money flowing in," Martin said.

"There's enough coming in now, but what about later in the year when the weather changes and there aren't as many visitors?" I asked.

"I guess attendance might go down slightly," Martin said.

"I expect a sixty percent decline in attendance from November to mid-March."

"Sixty percent?" my mother said. "That seems awfully pessimistic."

"Is it?" I said. "Do you think I just pulled those numbers out of my head?"

"No, I just thought that —"

"I went on the Net and checked out other zoos and exotic animal parks that operate in the same climate as us, and that was their *average* decline in attendance."

"I didn't know," my mother said. "I'm sorry."

"That's okay," I mumbled back. I usually felt bad right after I snapped at her, but it was even worse when she apologized. "It's just that we have to get financially ahead during the good weather so we have extra money we can use when attendance is down."

"And that's not happening?" my mother asked.

"We're just holding even."

"You can't be spending much on food," Martin said. "Those arrangements I made are sufficient, aren't they?"

"I'd hate to think what things would be like without those arrangements," I said.

"Then, other than feeding Vladimir — and I bet that costs a fortune — where's all the money going?" Nick asked.

"Veterinarian fees, medicine, and inoculations are expensive," I said, "but the real problem is the money that's going into building supplies to make all the new enclosures."

"How many new animals have been added?" Martin asked.

"Nine in the past three weeks, and judging from the phone calls I know of, there are others that are possibilities. It seems like everybody in the whole country has heard about Tiger Town and figures we can take in any exotic animal that no one else can care for."

"Mr. McCurdy can't take in every animal," Martin said.

"Thank you! That's what I keep saying to him! But does he listen to me? Mr. McCurdy just says it's a big farm and there's lots and lots of space left. It's not the space I'm worried about. It's the money."

"When it comes to animals, I'm afraid Angus thinks with his heart instead of his head," Martin agreed. "He loves his animals."

"He loves other people's animals, as well," I said, "even the ones he's never met. He feels like it's his job to rescue them, but it can't keep going on like this. He can't keep adding more and more animals."

"Do you think he'd ever sell off any of his animals?" Martin asked.

Nick burst into laughter. "Like that's going to happen."

"Actually, there was a guy there today talking about buying Kushna," I said.

"There was?" Nick asked, sounding shocked. Both Martin and my mother stared at me open-mouthed.

"Yeah, he was nosing around most of the day, making notes, and then he started talking about wanting to buy Kushna," I said.

"Why would anybody want to buy an old tiger?" my mother asked.

"There's only one reason I can think of," I said.

"Me, too," Nick agreed.

"You think he wanted to do something illegal with the tiger?" my mother asked.

"Only reason I can think of for wanting to buy him is to sell off the body parts," I said. "We all know how much a dead tiger's worth."

"It's still hard to believe somebody would sacrifice a tiger for a few dollars," my mother said.

"It's not a few dollars," I said. "Kushna's old, but he's big. They could get something like sixty or seventy thousand dollars. Between the bones, the organs, and the skin, he's worth a lot more dead than he ever was alive."

"That's just so barbaric," my mother said.

"It's barbaric and it's brought tigers to the brink of extinction," I said. "Do you know there are more tigers living in zoos around the world than there are living in the wild?"

"That's so sad," my mother said.

"It is," Martin agreed. "Almost as sad as what happened to that man."

"Man?" Nick asked. "What man?"

"The guy who wanted to buy the tiger," Martin said. "How far did he go when Vladimir threw him off the farm?"

"I didn't stay around to find out," I said.

"And it's better that I *never* find out," Martin said.

"I warned Vladimir he couldn't just pound the guy out," I said. "Even though he's now legally in the country, he still has to follow the law."

"That was wise of you to warn him," Martin said.

"He thinks because you two are friends you wouldn't arrest him. I told him it doesn't work that way in this country."

"I'd hate to have to arrest anybody who's a friend of mine — you can lose a lot of friends that way — but the law's the law."

"That's what I told him."

"But I don't think you have anything to worry about," Martin said.

"I don't?" Obviously, Martin didn't know Vladimir as well as he thought he did. I could picture Vladimir doing serious damage to that guy.

"Uh, no … I'd have heard if there was a problem — right?"

"I guess you would have."

"Besides, anybody who was trying to do something illegal like buying an exotic animal for slaughter would have to be pretty stupid to complain to the police if he was roughed up."

"He wasn't stupid," I said.

"How do you know that?" my mother asked.

I recognized that "mother" tone in her voice. I didn't really want to answer her question. She wouldn't be very happy if I told her it was all part of a plan to try to figure out what the guy wanted.

"Well?" my mother asked.

"I spoke to him a bit."

"That wasn't wise," she said.

"I didn't know what he wanted until I started talking to him and then once I found out I stopped."

"I remember reading that people involved in the illegal sale of exotic animals can be armed and dangerous," my mother said.

"Any illegal activity that involves large sums of money usually leads to danger and weapons," Martin said. "Did you know that the illegal trade in exotic animals is likely the second-largest smuggling activity after the drug trade?"

"I didn't know that," my mother said.

"It's estimated, and of course it can only be an estimate, that it involves up to ten billion dollars a year," Martin said.

"Ten billion dollars!" my mother said.

"I didn't believe it myself at first," Martin said, "but

I did some double-checking of facts and that was the number. That figure includes the sale of animal parts for traditional medicines, things like ivory from elephants, skin from alligators, fur from big cats, pets like tropical birds, reptiles, and other endangered animals, and ownership of large exotics like lions, tigers, and bears."

"Oh, *my*!" I said, quoting from *The Wizard of Oz*.

"There must be laws against these things," my mother, ever the lawyer, said.

"There's a patchwork of organizations and regulations that cover most of these things, but there's no fully coordinated international set of laws," Martin explained. "And while there are laws that regulate the importation or exportation of exotics in or out of the country, there's hardly any control over those that are born and raised here."

"And there's a lot of those," Nick said. "Tigers seem to breed like bunnies."

"Big bunnies with claws and teeth," Martin said. "These exotics pose a definite threat to the public."

"Not Mr. McCurdy's animals," I said, defending him.

"Even well-run places like his could have an escape," Martin said. "It does happen."

I knew what he was talking about. The summer before last Buddha had escaped. It was only by a combination of luck and skill that we were able to recapture him without anybody, including Buddha, getting hurt.

"For example," Martin said, "take that lion Mr. McCurdy got recently, the one that was the mascot for that motorcycle gang."

"Woody," I said.

"That's the one. While he was well cared for, as far as I've been told, he was still kept in a clubhouse with no bars. He could have slipped out the front door, and there's no telling what havoc he could have caused."

"He's very gentle," I said, now defending the lion.

"It doesn't matter how gentle he is," Martin said. "Would you want him to wander into a backyard where a toddler was playing in a sandbox?"

I shook my head. That was a scary thought.

"It was only because of a municipal bylaw that they couldn't keep it," Martin said.

"The same sort of bylaw that almost cost Mr. McCurdy his farm," Nick said.

"Similar," Martin agreed. "But that was the only law that got that lion away from that unsafe, poorly supervised situation. I'm not against well-supervised places where the animals are cared for by professionals —"

"Like Mr. McCurdy's place," I said.

"Like his place. I just think there has to be more done to protect the public and to regulate this massive illegal trade. There are magazines, websites, and public auctions where exotics are being bought and sold on a daily basis."

"I didn't know that," Nick said.

"Me, neither," my mother said.

"I didn't, either," I admitted. "But I was wondering, Martin. How do you know about all this stuff?"

The police chief's eyes widened ever so slightly, and he got that sort of look a kid gets when he's been caught in a lie — but, of course, I knew Martin wasn't lying.

"That's a good question," my mother said.

"I'm ... I'm the chief of police. I have to know about everything. It's part of my job."

"Knowing about exotic animals and the illegal trade is part of your job?" I asked.

"Of course it is, especially since we have Mr. McCurdy's place here," he said.

"I guess that makes sense," my mother said.

It did make sense, but there was something about the way Martin had looked that made me wonder if it made *complete* sense. Was there something he wasn't telling us?

"Just think," Martin said, "Angus is having money problems, but he has animals that are worth literally over a million dollars."

"That much?" Nick asked.

"Figure it out," Martin said. "The tigers alone are worth over a hundred and fifty thousand dollars. Throw in the jaguars, lions, leopards, the elephant, the black bear, and all the other animals and a million dollars is maybe a low estimate."

"But they're only worth that to the exotic animal traders, the people who want to slaughter the animals," I said.

"Of course," Martin said, "but for lots of people it would be tempting to make just one sale. The sale of one tiger would be enough to pay for all the other animals to live and to expand the farm to allow many other animals to be saved."

"You're not saying Angus should do that, are you?" my mother asked.

"Of course not," Martin said.

"Good, because there's no way he ever would," I said. "No way. He'd rather sacrifice himself than even one of those animals."

"I'm sure you're right," Martin said.

"I *know* I'm right."

Martin got up from the table and picked up his now-empty plate. "That was, as always, a wonderful meal. Thank you."

"You're welcome," both my mother and I said. I didn't know why she had said thanks, since I was the one who had fixed most of the meal.

"I hate to eat and run, but I better get going," Martin said. "I was thinking I should take a little spin over to see Angus and Vladimir. Just to make sure everything's okay."

"That sounds like a good idea," my mother said.

I wasn't certain it *was* such a good idea. Maybe I should have kept my mouth shut and not mentioned the stranger to anybody. But good or bad, it was done.

Chapter 7

Quickly, I walked down the laneway to Tiger Town. My body had been in school all day, but my head had been here at the animal farm. In part I was thinking about Kanga and Roo. Another part was wondering what had happened to the stranger, though I was pretty sure I knew the answer to that. I just hoped Vladimir hadn't done anything that might get him into trouble. And while I was worried about that, something else was preoccupying me. I was thinking about a conversation I wanted to have with Mr. McCurdy and Vladimir. I wanted to sit them both down and have a long, hard, serious talk about not getting more animals for Tiger Town. It just couldn't go on like this, adding animal after animal.

I wanted to explain to them that they had to think of Tiger Town as a big boat — like Noah's Ark. And all boats, no matter how big, could hold only so many animals. Heck, Noah took a pair of every animal, but he didn't take *every* animal. There was a limit to how many animals any boat — or farm — could handle.

And if you tried to put more animals on a boat than it could handle, the boat would eventually sink. Instead of saving all the animals you'd save no animals. That made sense ... didn't it?

I'd sit those two down and talk logically, making sense, explaining everything so they could see that what I was saying was right. The big problem, of course, was that sometimes their passion, their love of animals, got in the way of their thinking. At those times they didn't even want to listen to logic because their minds were already made up. If they weren't both such nice guys — wonderful guys — I'd get mad at them.

I entered the farmhouse. "Hello!"

Calvin came running down the hall toward me, using his arms to propel him, a big smile on his face. I knew what was going to come next, and I also knew I was helpless to stop it from happening.

The chimp threw his arms into the air, wrapped them around my neck, and pulled me over until my head was at the same level as his. He then planted a big, loud, sloppy kiss right on my forehead!

"Calvin!" I screamed. "Let me go!"

He released me from his vise-like grip, and I straightened back up. I wiped away the ape slobber from my face — at least he hadn't kissed me on the mouth this time.

"I wish you wouldn't do that," I said.

The smile on Calvin's face faded, and he looked sad. Oh, great, I'd hurt the chimp's feelings. Now I felt bad. I didn't like him kissing me because it was a bad combination of stale banana breath and saliva, but I knew he only kissed people he liked, so it was sort of an honour really. Maybe it would be better if I just put up with it and didn't say anything. Sort of the way I put up with my great-aunts kissing me when we went to family gatherings. Either way I didn't have much choice. There was family pressure to let my aunties kiss me and a pressure of a different kind involved with Calvin's kiss … the sort of pressure that involved an animal so strong that he could actually rip an arm right out of its socket.

"Calvin," I said, "I'm sorry. If you want to kiss me, that's okay."

He peered up at me, and his expression changed as he began to smile again. That was nice. I was glad he understood and that he was happy. Then Calvin put a finger against his nose, spread out his other hairy fingers, and went *"Ppplllllllzzzzzzzz!"* A mist of saliva shot into the air. He threw back his head, howled with laughter, and raced back down the hall toward the kitchen.

Great! I'd just been rejected by a chimpanzee. The only good thing was that my brother hadn't been around to witness it. I followed Calvin, but when I walked into the kitchen, I stopped dead in my tracks. There, sitting at the table, was that man!

"What … what are you doing here?" I asked, my voice barely louder than a whisper.

He smiled, but it wasn't a friendly smile. It was the sort of smile the big bad wolf gave to Goldilocks. Lots of teeth and no sincerity.

"Answer me," I demanded. "Why are you here?" I was shocked that I was so bold.

"I guess I could ask you the same question," the stranger said. He stood up and suddenly seemed much bigger here in the confines of the kitchen. So much for feeling bold or brave. I took a half-step backwards.

"I just want to know where Mr. McCurdy is," I said, my voice cracking over the last few words.

"Not far," he said, taking a couple of steps toward me.

Terrified, I retreated the same number of steps. "Don't you come any closer!"

"Closer?" he asked. He sounded confused ... no, not confused, *amused*. "I'm only going closer to the *fridge* to get another soda. You don't have any objections to me approaching the fridge, do you?" He walked to the fridge, opened the door, and pulled out a Coke. "Do you want one?" He held the can out toward me.

"The only thing I want from you is to tell me where Mr. McCurdy is." I took a few small steps backwards, just barely sliding my feet along the floor. I wanted to be close enough to the door to run outside and escape if he tried to get me. "What have you done with Mr. McCurdy?"

"Me?" he asked. "I've done nothing *to* Mr. McCurdy." He started walking toward me.

I turned and banged into the wall, bounced off, then raced for the front door. I had to get out before the stranger could catch me. Hurling open the door, I bumped into Vladimir. I bounced back and then the swinging door shut and hit me. I was shocked by Vladimir's sudden appearance, but relieved — he was here and could protect me!

"Big girl Sarah okay? Didn't mean to hurt!"

"He's here! He's here!" I practically screamed.

"Who where?" Vladimir sounding worried.

"That man ... that man from yesterday!"

His worried expression dissolved into a smile. "You mean Anthony?"

"I don't know what his name is … but you do … and you're not worried, are you?"

"Not worried. Vladimir know Anthony here."

"But why is he here?" I demanded. "He wanted to buy Kushna … he wanted to slaughter him!"

Vladimir laughed. "Not really want buy Kushna. Just pretend."

"Pretend? Why would he pretend that?"

"Hard to explain. Come inside and meet Anthony."

"I don't want to meet him," I said.

"Be nice, big girl Sarah. Anthony nice man."

"How can he be nice?"

"Is nice. You see. Come, meet Anthony," he said.

Before I could answer, Vladimir took me by the hand and led me inside. Trying to resist Vladimir would be basically impossible, but there was no reason he'd bring me back inside if there was any danger. We walked down the hall and into the kitchen. This man — this Anthony — was sitting at the table. Calvin was now sitting at the table, as well, right beside him. They were both drinking Cokes.

"Glad you decided to come back," Anthony said.

"It wasn't my idea," I said.

"Anthony, tell Sarah why you talk about Kushna," Vladimir said.

"Certainly. Please sit." With his foot he pushed out the chair directly across from him.

Reluctantly, against my better judgment, I sat down.

"I needed to ask about buying an animal and hint that I was going to do something bad with it to see if

Angus and Vladimir would sell it to me," Anthony said.

"Huh?"

"I was testing them," he said.

"Testing them? What does that mean?"

"I'd heard they were good people who cared about their animals, but I had to be sure they weren't into anything illegal with their animals."

"If you knew them at all, you'd know they'd never do anything like that," I said.

"That's the thing. I didn't know them. I had to find out for myself. I had to test them."

"So you said all that stuff to test them?"

He nodded. "Exactly. Now do you understand?"

"I understand, but it's still awful," I said. "You can't just go around playing tricks on people!"

"Tricks? You mean the way you came up and talked to me and tried to trick me into telling you who I was and what I was writing in my notebook?"

"That's different," I said.

"How?"

"Well ... I wasn't really trying to trick you or test you."

"You're right," he agreed. "What you were doing was more like spying."

"I was just trying to find out what you were up to, that's all," I said.

"The way I was trying to find out what Angus and Vladimir were up to. Were they caring people or were they running a place where animals could be bought and sold for body parts for profit. I had to know."

I didn't know what to say. Maybe he was right. Perhaps he hadn't done anything that different from what I had done. "I guess I'm sorry," I said. "I didn't mean to trick you."

Anthony laughed. "No fear there. I figured out what you were up to the moment you opened your mouth. You're not, how should I say this, a very good actress."

"I never said I was."

"Some people just aren't meant to lie," he said.

"Big girl Sarah very, *very* bad liar," Vladimir said.

"I'd hate to rely on your ability to lie to anybody," Anthony said.

"I guess I'm not a very good liar because I haven't had much practice," I said defensively. "Usually, I just tell the truth."

"Sometimes there's no choice," Anthony said. "I had to lie to find out the truth. There was no way I was going to invest unless I was one hundred percent certain."

"Invest?"

He smiled. "Here, in Tiger Town. You asked why I was here. I'm still here because I'm the newest partner."

"I … I don't understand," I said.

"Easy to understand," Vladimir said. "Anthony give money to run place, build more pens, get more animals."

"Why would he want to do that?" I asked, dumbfounded.

"Because by becoming a partner I get a percentage of the profits from Tiger Town," Anthony said.

"Profits? What profits?" I said before I could even think to stop myself. I shouldn't have said that.

"There will be profits," Anthony said. "It will take a lot of work and a lot of money, but once I get this place up and running the right way it will make money. Sometimes you have to spend money to make money."

"Is not wonderful news?" Vladimir asked enthusiastically.

"Yeah, great news, great," I said. It did sound like good news. That's what my head said. My stomach gave a different answer.

Chapter 8

I wandered between the rows of new pens. It was the Tiger Town I knew and loved, but it was different, so very different. The changes had been sudden, shocking, and surprising. We'd been studying alliteration at school, and I found it fascinating, fun, and phenomenal — did that last one count because it started with a *ph* but did make the *f* sound? Maybe Nick was right. I *did* like school too much.

It had been nonstop construction for a week. The work had started the day after Anthony arrived and hadn't stopped, or shown any signs of stopping. Stacks of construction materials were still lying around, and there were lots of men — people I'd never met — converting these materials into pens, reconstructing the snack bar, repairing the barn, and generally improving the grounds. There was a constant barrage of pounding hammers punctuated by the roaring, squealing sound of saws ripping into wood. I wondered if all the noise disturbed the animals as much as it bothered me. Mr. McCurdy said they'd get used to it. He was probably right, but either way it was happening.

So far eight new pens had been constructed. The new lion had one, while a second was home to our latest leopard. A third was home to a tiger that had just sort of magically appeared one day when I was at school. I hadn't heard anything about it coming and then it was just there. A fourth pen was waiting for the kangaroos — who were now living in the spare bedroom in the farmhouse — to get old enough to be outside and on their own. The others were empty, though I suspected they wouldn't stay vacant for long. At least that's what Anthony had said. "Trust me," he'd told me. "There'll be animals in them soon."

I *believed* him, but I certainly didn't *trust* him. There was something about somebody saying *trust me* or *honestly* that made me *not* trust them and think that something *dis*honest was happening.

So far there was nothing I could really put my finger on. He'd done what he'd said he was going to do. He had pumped in a lot of money to improve the place. It was more the way he acted. He was always ordering people around as if he were the boss. I guess with the workmen he was the boss, but he seemed to be giving orders to Mr. McCurdy and Vladimir, as well. Mr. McCurdy owned the farm, and Vladimir didn't need to take orders from anybody. The strange thing was that they appeared to be doing what he told them to do. And while they were working Anthony just sort of stood there, off to the side, often half hidden in the shadows, watching. He had this way of looking at people as if he were judging them or trying to figure them out. It was unnerving!

A couple of times he'd almost caught me staring at him, trying to figure him out. I'd managed to glance away quickly enough so that he hadn't noticed.

But what really bothered me the most — and this was almost stupid — were Anthony's shoes. I guess they weren't shoes, but boots. Pointy toes, heels, shiny boots that extended up and under his jeans. He was always rubbing the top of one against the back of the other pant leg or bending down and rubbing them with a handkerchief he had in his back pocket. And those boots weren't made of leather. It was some sort of fancy material ... like the skin of a snake or reptile or something. I wasn't going to ask. It just seemed really strange that somebody who said he was so interested in the welfare of animals would so proudly wear the skin of some dead animal.

Actually, come to think of it, I'd seen Anthony observing the animals, making notes, supervising the construction of new pens, talking about the animals, but I'd never really seen him appear that interested in the animals themselves. I'd never seen him "cooing" over the kangaroos, or petting Laura the cheetah, or talking to Calvin. He even seemed nervous around Calvin. And I'd noticed that Calvin wasn't offering to kiss him. That chimp was a good judge of people, I thought.

The only good thing about those boots of Anthony's was that they made a very distinctive sound. I could always hear his heels against the gravel, which was my cue to make tracks.

"Hey, Sarah!"

I turned around. It was Nick ... accompanied by Anthony. As much as I disliked Anthony, it seemed that Nick liked him. Then again I just wished Nick was as good a *judge* of character as he *was* a character. I stood there waiting for them.

"You should see Tiger Town's website," Nick said.

"Tiger Town has a website?" I said. "I didn't even know we had a computer."

"We have both now," Anthony said. "State-of-the-art, top-of-the-line in both cases. We need to communicate with zoos, game farms, private collectors, and animal dealers around the world."

"I guess that makes sense," I agreed reluctantly.

"Everything's major high-tech, especially the cameras," Nick said.

"What cameras?" I asked.

Anthony put a finger to his lips to silence me. "We don't want people to know, but we've had surveillance cameras installed."

"I haven't seen any cameras."

"That's because we've camouflaged them," Anthony explained. "I can see at least three of them from where we're standing. Can you figure out where they are?"

I looked around, first in one direction, then the other. I didn't see anything that even remotely seemed like a camera.

"That probably wasn't fair," Anthony said. "They aren't visible at all, even if you know where to look. They're hidden in the new lights that have been installed."

I glanced at the nearest light. A series of lampposts had been newly installed along the paths. They really did look nice. "Why do we need cameras?" I asked.

"So we can safeguard our animals," Anthony said. "We can't be everywhere at once, but with the cameras we have extra eyes to make sure nobody does any harm to the animals, including things like opening up the cages. We don't want Buddha out and about again."

"I guess that makes sense," I said, "but why are the cameras hidden? It feels like we're spying on people."

"The cameras are aimed at the animals and they're hidden because people get uncomfortable when they think they're being watched," Anthony explained.

"I know *I* am," I said.

"And people who are uncomfortable tend not to return. We need our customers, our visitors, to make many return visits."

"And you think we can get enough visitors to pay for all this new stuff?" I asked.

"They'll pay for part of it. The visitors are only one stream of revenue."

"Stream of revenue?"

"It's a business term. It means that money, income, revenue, comes from different sources, different *streams.*"

"Oh, you mean like we make money from selling the ice-cream bars," I said.

He chuckled. "Like all the things that will be sold at the *new* snack bar. But that's just one trickle as opposed to a stream."

"Then what are the other streams?" I asked.

"The major source will involve the sale of animals."

"What?" I gasped. "We can't sell animals!"

"Of course we can. We will."

"Mr. McCurdy will never agree to that."

"He will and he has," Anthony said. "Do you think I'm doing all of this behind his back? All game farms buy, sell, and trade animals continually. I know Mr. McCurdy bought and sold animals during his time working for the circus."

"I'm sure he *bought* animals," I shot back.

"What do you think he did with all the animals he bred?" Anthony asked.

I hadn't thought about that. I knew Mr. McCurdy had had a lot of success breeding and raising all sorts of animals, and they all couldn't have stayed with the circus.

"Everything will be done with legitimate zoos and game farms, people committed to caring for animals," Anthony said.

"Oh, that's good," I said.

"You sound surprised by that. Did you think we were going to sell them to illegal traders?"

"Of course not," I lied. I wasn't sure what Anthony had in mind.

"There would be a lot more money in illegal sales, as we all know, but if we selectively buy, breed, rescue, and rehabilitate animals, we can make this farm profitable. Take those kangaroos, for example."

"What about Kanga and Roo?" I asked.

"The farm got the two kangaroos for free. If those two can be successfully raised, they can be sold for close to ten thousand dollars each."

"You want to sell my kangaroos?"

"First off, the kangaroos belong to Tiger Town. Second, there are no plans to sell the kangaroos at this time."

I felt better.

"Quite frankly, the kangaroos are simply not marketable at this time," Anthony said. "They're still too young, require far too much care, and might not even survive to adulthood."

"Kanga and Roo are going to live!"

"I certainly hope so," he said. "It would be *awful* if something happened to them."

That was nice — and unexpected — of him to say that. Maybe I'd really been misjudging him, had been too hard on him. After all, he did like the —

"Dead animals mean lost money, and we're going to work to make this place profitable," he said.

So much for that thought.

"There are, of course, some animals that would never be sold," Anthony continued. "For example, Laura and Calvin, Polly, Kushna, and Buddha."

"I hope not. They're pets."

"They're also not worth anything."

"How can you say that?" I asked, feeling offended.

"It's a fact. They're all too old and have far too many bad habits to be worth anything to anybody except Angus or Vladimir. In fact, the only value Calvin would have is as a laboratory subject."

"What does that mean?" I asked, not knowing but definitely not liking the sound of it.

"Research labs are always looking for primates to pursue scientific research," Anthony explained. "They test new medicines and surgical procedures and —"

"That's so inhumane!"

"That's why they don't use humans," Anthony said. "But Calvin's safe. The only thing he'd be good for is the Pepsi challenge to see which soft drink really does taste the best."

Nick laughed at Anthony's little attempt at a joke.

"Mr. McCurdy wouldn't sell Calvin for a million dollars," I insisted.

"You're correct, and that's where he went wrong."

I gave him a questioning and angry glare.

"If you get too close to the animals, make them into pets, you can't make the right business decisions regarding the animals."

"But maybe the best thing you can do is to get close to the animals," I argued. "Why would you be involved in something like this if you didn't like animals?"

He smirked. "Remind me never to become a business partner of yours."

Nick chuckled again. He was really becoming a little suck-up. I knew how to push that laughter back down his throat.

"Are you going to sell Peanuts?" I asked.

"Peanuts?" Nick yelped.

I saw the colour drain from his face. I knew how much he loved that elephant, and it was mean of me even to suggest selling Peanuts. "I figure a big animal like that must be worth a lot of money," I said.

"More than the kangaroos," Anthony said. "But the elephant will be staying right here."

I could see the relief on Nick's face. "I don't understand," I said. "You'd sell the kangaroos, but you won't sell Peanuts. Why?"

"I have other ideas in mind for the elephant," Anthony said.

"What sort of ideas?" I asked, thinking about ivory traders and the elephant's tusks.

"Did you know that a baby elephant is worth between thirty and fifty thousand dollars?" Anthony asked.

"Yeah, but Peanuts isn't a baby."

"But he could help to produce babies."

"That would be pretty hard to do on his own, don't you think?" I said.

"I'm glad you understand the basics of reproduction. We have enough space on this farm to support a whole *herd* of elephants. A whole herd that could form a breeding stock to produce lots of little elephants."

"That would be incredible!" Nick said. "Just incredible! Wait until Peanuts sees that he's got friends."

"Speaking of Peanuts, have you cleaned his pen today?" I asked.

"Well, not yet."

"You know that's one of your jobs and it needs to be done."

"It's a big job," Nick said, "because elephants *do* big jobs. It can wait until tomorrow."

"I think your sister's right, Nick," Anthony said. Judging by the look on my brother's face, he was as surprised as I was that Anthony was agreeing with something I had said. "Visitors don't like messy pens, and I noticed that the elephant pen does need attention. Besides, if we can't count on your help with *one* elephant, what will happen when there are *many* elephants?"

That was a good point. Maybe shovelling elephant dung for the day would dampen Nick's enthusiasm about a whole herd living here.

"As well, it will give me a chance to talk to Sarah," Anthony added.

I straightened up. What did he want to talk to me about? Whatever it was I really didn't want to speak to him. I'd spent the better part of the past week deliberately working at not talking to him.

"If that's all right with you, Sarah," Anthony said.

"Why wouldn't it be?" I asked.

"I don't know. It just seems like you're always trying to avoid me."

"I wouldn't do that," I lied.

He smiled — that sick, smirky smile of his that without words said he knew I was lying.

"Okay, then I better get going," Nick said, walking off.

"So, Sarah, I was hoping to get your opinion," Anthony said when Nick was out of earshot.

"You want my opinion?" I asked.

He nodded. "Your opinion's important to me."

"Well," I began, "there certainly have been a lot of changes to improve Tiger Town."

"That's not what I want your opinion on. I want to know what you think about me."

"About you?"

"Yes, tell me your insights and assessment of me."

I didn't answer. I didn't know what to say. I knew what I thought of him, but I couldn't really say that.

"Come, come, Sarah, I've seen you watching me and I know you well enough to figure you have an opinion. I'd like to hear it."

He stared straight at me, his arms folded across his chest, that smirk getting even larger.

"Well, I guess at the very beginning I was a little bit uneasy about —"

"Sarah, before you continue, please remember that you are, without a doubt, the *worst* liar I've ever met in my entire life. So I suggest that rather than embarrass us both that you simply tell me your real opinion."

I felt stunned. What was I supposed to say now? I stood silently.

"If you can't say anything good, don't say anything at all, huh?" His smirk grew bigger again. "You probably don't think I have feelings, so there's no danger of you hurting them." He lifted his left foot and rubbed the toe of his boot against the back of the other leg. "Just go ahead and spit it out."

"I don't like you!" I snapped, the words jumping out before I could stop myself.

His smirk softened into a smile. "I suppose you don't trust me at all, either."

"Not as far as I can throw you."

"And you don't think I even like animals."

"You like money and the animals are nothing more than money to you!"

"Further, you hate these boots," he said, gesturing at his shiny, shorn feet.

I nodded enthusiastically.

"They're very comfortable. Do you know what they're made of?"

This time I shook my head.

"It's caiman. I don't imagine you even know what a caiman is."

"It's like an alligator from South America. Some types are very rare and endangered."

"Actually, *these* are made from a very rare type."

I shuddered. I wasn't surprised, but I was still offended.

"Now I'd like to tell you what I think of you," Anthony said.

I didn't care what he thought of me, but I still didn't

want to hear it. What awful thing was he going to say about me? I braced myself.

"I like you."

"Yeah, right," I scoffed.

"I do. And the reason I like you is because you remind me very much of a younger version of me."

I was expecting him to insult me, but this was really hitting below the belt.

"And I'll tell you why," he continued. "You and I are both, by nature, very observant and very analytical. We're both always trying to figure out what's going on around us. Watching, observing, predicting, trying to foresee every possible consequence and then strategizing how to handle them all."

I remained silent. Just because that was how I was didn't mean I had to agree with him.

"You're very smart and do well, *very* well, in school. Partially, that's because you're clever, but also, partially, it's because you simply outwork everybody else. And finally, you not only want, but you need, to be in control. It bothers you when somebody else is in control, and that's perhaps why you don't like me."

"There could be lots of reasons why I don't like you," I added.

"Regardless, I still like you. I even admire you." He paused. "Of course, that doesn't mean I'm going to let you get in the way of what needs to be done. Remember that."

He turned and walked away, and I felt an eerie chill spread throughout my entire body.

Chapter 9

I opened up the freezer. The new freezer. It was packed to the rim with meat. Anthony had not only bought a new freezer but he'd worked out some deal with a meat packer so we could get all of the meat we needed. It came pre-packaged, all wrapped up in brown paper, labelled, and weighed. I wondered how much he was paying for the meat, but it really didn't matter. There seemed to be enough money for everything.

Everything included the two men who had been hired to help around the farm. Their names were Bob and Doug, and they were doing a whole lot of the work involving the cleaning of pens and feeding the animals. I still helped out with Buddha and Kushna, but that was because I liked to. The only job that was mine to do most of the time was the feeding of Kanga and Roo. They had gotten so much bigger and stronger over the past seven weeks. They'd let other people feed them — and that was wonderful because I couldn't be there every day and every night for every feeding — but when they saw me coming they ignored everybody else completely. I was proud of my little joeys.

Nick was pretty happy letting the two men do most of the work. He spent a great deal of his time playing with or riding Peanuts. My brother loved that elephant and couldn't wait until more elephants appeared.

It was funny, but the first time I'd met the two new men I didn't think I'd like them. Partly because they were hired by Anthony and partly because they both actually looked like him. They had the same short hair, stiff backs, and muscular builds as he did. To be honest, though, they actually resembled the way he *used* to look rather than the way he appeared now.

In the time since Anthony had arrived he'd let his hair grow and he now sported a funny little goatee on his face. I never trusted anybody with a goatee. On his head he had a big black Stetson, which made him look like the bad guy in a bad western. And now he almost always wore a pair of dark-tinted sunglasses. He even wore them when it wasn't sunny outside or when he was sitting at the kitchen table in the farmhouse. You couldn't see his eyes, or where he was looking, but I knew those dark eyes were scanning the room, planning, plotting, scheming.

I'd tried to talk to Mr. McCurdy and Vladimir about what I was thinking, but it was clear they really didn't want to know. They were busy and happy, and it probably wasn't right to bother or worry them when I really didn't have any solid reasons to support my worries. Talking to Nick was useless — even more useless than usual. He liked Anthony and was just waiting for the new elephants to start arriving.

When I finally spoke to my mother, she played her lawyer role. It was as if I were being questioned on the witness stand. She cross-examined me to see what evidence I had to support my beliefs. She wanted the facts and nothing but the facts. But, of course, there weren't any. Since Anthony had come, there were more animals, better pens, no worries about food or the future, and the attendance had actually risen instead of doing what I'd predicted. I didn't like being wrong, even when it meant good news.

My mother even had the nerve to suggest that since Anthony had arrived everything was being taken care of and maybe that was why I didn't like him — because I wasn't needed as much. I got so mad when she said that. What I really needed was a mother who would listen to me instead of treating me like part of a court proceeding. She was in the middle of some big trial and, like always, she got more "lawyerly" when that was happening.

"Sarah!" Nick yelled. "Did you see the big truck that just arrived?"

"If it just arrived and I'm here, what do you think?"

"Just asking. It's an animal truck with lots of cages inside."

"Are there any animals in those cages?" I asked.

"Empty," he said. "I looked inside. What do you think that means?"

It seemed pretty obvious to me. If the truck was empty, it was perhaps coming here to get filled.

"Strange thing," Nick said. "I saw the driver get out of the truck, and he looked familiar to me."

"He did?"

Nick nodded. "And it's bugging me that I know I know him, but I just can't figure out where or why."

"Where is he now?" I asked.

"I'm not sure. He and Anthony went off together."

"He knows Anthony?"

"Looked like it. Either that or he came here to meet with him."

Anybody who knew Anthony or was here to meet him made me uneasy. "I was thinking that if you think you know this guy, then maybe I know him, too," I said. "If you showed him to me, I might be able to solve the mystery." I wanted to see what was going on. Maybe I was my mother's daughter because I was looking for evidence.

"That makes sense," Nick said.

I closed the door of the freezer. "Where do you think they might be now?"

"Could be anywhere, but I know how we can find out. Come with me."

"Where are we going?"

"To the place with the best view in Tiger Town," Nick said.

"We're going to the silo?"

He laughed. "The control room."

I hadn't been in there, but Nick had told me that the control room was where all the cameras fed back their pictures.

"Those cameras see almost all of the farm," Nick said.

"But won't it be locked?" I asked.

"It's always locked. There are tens of thousands of dollars of equipment in there."

"Then it's not going to do us any good to go there."

"I said it was locked. I didn't say I didn't know the combination to get in. Let's go."

I trailed Nick out of the stable and around the side of the barn. He cut between two pens, each holding a jaguar. There were pairs of green eyes staring at us from both sides as we moved down the narrow aisle between the enclosures. I knew neither cat could get out to pounce on us, but I wondered if either could hook out a paw far enough between the bars to take a little swipe as we passed.

"I can't wait until we get another elephant," Nick said. "That's why I went to check out the truck. It was big enough to hold an elephant."

Or take one away, I thought, but kept silent. "You went to check out the truck because you're nosy," I said.

"That, too. Vladimir said he'll even let me help train the new ones."

"That's exciting," I agreed. Assuming there were going to be other elephants. Then again, why did I doubt Anthony? It wasn't as if animals didn't keep appearing. At last count — and that count changed regularly — we had added four tigers, two lions, a bear, some gazelles, and over two dozen parrots. He'd said that parrots were going to increase our "revenue stream" dramatically.

I thought it would have been nice to let Polly play with or talk to the new parrots, but he wasn't allowed. Anthony said he was protecting Polly from possible "infections" that the new birds might be carrying. I thought it had more to do with the fact that he didn't want Polly to "infect" the new birds with any of his language.

Nick stopped at the door of the control room. It was at the back end of the new snack bar. The building had been finished three weeks ago, and I'd never been in either part of it. Nick bent over and punched some numbers into the keypad. The door beeped and then popped open. Nick pushed it open, and I followed him inside.

I stopped dead in my tracks. I didn't know what I'd expected, but this wasn't it. On the wall was a bank of television screens, six in all, showing different views of Tiger Town!

"Pretty impressive, huh?" Nick asked.

"Pretty scary. I knew there were cameras. I just didn't know how much they were watching." My eyes jumped from one screen to the next to the next. "But I don't see Anthony on any of the screens."

"We'll just have to look around a little." Nick sat down on a chair in front of a big control console underneath the screens. He pushed a button, and one of the screens changed to a different scene. Nick continued to hit buttons, and the different screens switched to different views.

There had to be dozens and dozens of cameras. It was amazing ... and troubling. Why would anybody want that many cameras?

"There they are," Nick said, pointing up at one of the screens.

I moved closer, but the figures were so small that I couldn't make out much of anything. If it wasn't for that big black cowboy hat, I wouldn't have been able to tell it was Anthony, so I certainly couldn't make out the features of the other man to see if I knew him. They were standing in front of the pen of one of the new tigers.

I'd asked Anthony what the tiger's name was, and he had told me it didn't have one and that it wasn't necessarily going to be around long enough for us to give him one. Was this guy a potential buyer?

"Does he look familiar to you?" Nick asked.

"Familiar? From what I can see I can hardly tell he's the same species as us. Let's go and have a closer look."

"We can have a closer look without going anywhere." Nick reached over and turned a knob on the console, and as he twisted it, the camera zoomed in closer and closer until the images of the two men filled the screen. "Is that better?"

"If seeing more of Anthony is better, then it's a whole lot better."

"I don't know why you don't like him," Nick said.

"How much time do you have? Because it'll take a long time to explain it."

"I've got no time to waste listening to you. So just tell me. Do you think that guy looks familiar? Do you know who he is?"

I'd been focusing so much on my bad feelings about Anthony that I'd forgotten why we were here in the first place. I turned my attention to the screen.

The other man was older and heavy-set. He wore a white safari suit — the kind you see people wear on those animal television shows where they track wild beasts or play with poisonous snakes or crocodiles. His hair was thinning and his face was bloated. His skin seemed to glisten as if it were oily.

"He looks *so* familiar," Nick said. "Does he look familiar to you?"

"He looks like a whole bunch of people who — oh, my goodness!" I gasped. "I *do* know who he is."

"You do? That's great! So who is he?"

As I watched, the stranger and Anthony both broke into smiles and shook hands as if they'd come to some sort of agreement. If that man was who I thought he was, that agreement could mean the death of one of the tigers.

"Sarah!" Nick said, tapping me on the arm and breaking me out of my trance.

"Yeah?"

"You said you know who he is."

"I do and I think I know why he's here."

"Why? Why is he here?" Nick asked.

"He's come to buy one of the tigers … so he can slaughter it."

Chapter 10

"Sarah, where are you going?" Nick demanded.

"I'm going to save the tiger!" I yelled over my shoulder as I ran from the control room. "We have to find Vladimir and Mr. McCurdy!"

"Sarah, stop!"

"There's no time to —" I was suddenly halted in my tracks and spun around as Nick grabbed my arm.

"We better have time, because I have no idea what you're talking about and we're not going anywhere until you tell me. Who is that man and why do you think the tiger's in danger?"

For a second I thought about shaking Nick off, breaking free, and running away, but I didn't have time to fight him right now. It was better to explain quickly. "Let go of my arm and I'll tell you."

He released his grip.

"You recognize that man from last summer," I said.

"I met lots of people last summer, but I don't think he was one of them."

"I didn't say you met him, but you did see him at

the Armstrong animal camp." Nick and I had spent a week at an exotic animal camp — a present from our father. He thought that because of all the contact we'd had with Mr. McCurdy and his animals that we'd just naturally want to go to that camp. We'd gone. What we'd found was a rundown place with animals on the verge of being sold off into illegal trade. Through the help of Vladimir — the one employee of the camp — and Mr. McCurdy, we were able to foil the plans of the owners and rescue the animals. Many of those animals had come with Vladimir when he started working with Mr. McCurdy.

"The only men I remember from last summer are Vladimir and that awful Mr. Armstrong," Nick said.

Mr. Armstrong and his wife had inherited the camp from his father. He didn't like animals. And the only things his wife had seemed to like were new shoes. Mr. Armstrong had kept selling off the animals to pay for her shopping sprees.

"And unless Mr. Armstrong gained a lot of weight, lost most of his hair, and got thirty years older in two months, this guy isn't him," Nick said.

"It isn't Mr. Armstrong, but you saw him when he was *with* Mr. Armstrong."

"I did?"

"It was at night and it was dark."

"Isn't it usually dark at night, Sarah?" Nick asked.

"Shut up, quit being such a smart aleck, and think!" I snapped.

"I still don't —"

"That's the guy who was trying to buy Kushna so he could kill him and sell off the body parts!"

Nick's eyes widened and his mouth opened, but he didn't say anything. Wow, Nick shocked into silence. Where was a camera when you needed one?

Finally, he spoke. "Sarah ... are you positive?"

"Not a million percent, but I know it's him. I'm positive ... almost completely."

"It was dark and it was just in the headlights of the car and we didn't see him for long and we weren't even that close," Nick said.

"Long enough, close enough, and enough light for you to recognize him and for me to see and remember him."

"Enough of all of that for me to think that *maybe* I recognized him," Nick said. "But that doesn't mean I recognized him from there."

"It's *him* and it's from *there*," I said, stressing my words. "And that means he can only be here for one reason. We have to get Mr. McCurdy and Vladimir and we have to stop him."

I turned away with the intention of moving again, but Nick grabbed my arm once more to stop me. "What are you doing?" I demanded.

"I'm stopping you from making a total fool of yourself."

"What?"

"You think that everybody is up to no good with these animals. You're getting paranoid about everything."

"I'm not getting paranoid about anything!" I shouted.

"Aren't you? What about Anthony? You think he's bad and you see him shaking hands with this guy, so you figure he's bad, too, and then your mind clicks back to a bad guy who looks like this guy. You put two and two together and you get five."

"Are you crazy?" I gasped.

"I'm not the one making strange connections and leaping to wild conclusions," Nick said.

I opened my mouth to argue, then stopped myself. I knew there was nothing I could say to convince Nick. His mind was made up, and it was such a tiny place that there wasn't much room for facts or information. Actually, I didn't have any more facts or information. But I knew I was right. I was positive. *Completely* positive. Well, *almost* completely positive. Nick had planted a seed of doubt in my mind.

"Nick, I want you to listen to me very closely."

"I'm listening."

"First, I know you don't believe me, but believe *this*. If you don't remove your hand from my arm, I'm going to break it off."

Nick looked shocked, but his hand stayed put.

"Now!" I yelled, and Nick let go. "Second, I don't care if you don't believe me because you're still going to do what I tell you to do."

"And what's that?"

"You're going up to the farmhouse and find Mr. McCurdy and Vladimir — that's where they were headed the last time I talked to them. And you're going to tell them there's an emergency and get them down to the tiger pens as quickly as possible."

"And what are you going to be doing while I'm doing that?"

"I'm going straight to the pens. I'm going to delay

things, maybe even explain to Anthony who this guy is and —"

"Who you *think* he is," Nick said, cutting me off.

"Who I *know* he is."

"Sarah, you need to stop and think things through a second time before you do anything."

"This coming from you?" I cried. "The king of act first, think never?"

"Especially coming from me. I've had lots of practice being wrong. Do you know how much trouble you're going to be in if you're wrong?"

"Not as much trouble as that tiger is going to be in if I'm right and we don't do anything."

Nick didn't answer right away. That meant he was thinking. That probably meant he knew we had no choice. "Okay, I'll go, but you make sure when this explodes in our faces that everybody knows that none of this was my idea."

"I'll explain everything to them if you just hurry."

"I'll hurry. After all, it's not every day that it's you who looks like an idiot instead of me." He turned and began to run off.

"Nick!" I yelled. He skidded to a stop and turned around. "Tell Mr. McCurdy to bring his gun." Nick nodded, then started off again.

I ran in the other direction. It was a good distance from here to the far side of the barn. I just hoped I wasn't too late. I had to get there in time. Of course, what was I going to say when I did arrive? At least I was reassured to know that while I'd seen this man before he'd never seen me. I had been hiding in the trees in the dark, so he'd never seen my face. He probably didn't even know I existed. I just had to slow things down, sort of get in the way so Anthony and the man couldn't talk or conclude any business before Mr. McCurdy arrived. If worst came to worst, I'd just pull Anthony to the side, tell him I had something very personal to talk to him about, and explain it. It would be worth it to see that smug little smile wiped off his face. That is, if he believed me. It was a pretty wild story … unless he already knew who this guy was. I put on the brakes.

My mind was filled with a terrible thought. Maybe Anthony would have no difficulty believing me because he already knew who this guy was and why he was here and he was part of it. Perhaps this was the evidence I'd needed that he was up to no good himself and was planning on selling the tiger for body parts. That was how he was going to pay for all those expensive gadgets and still make a profit!

What was he going to say when I barged in and tried to put a stop to his business and cost him tens of thousands of dollars? He'd already warned me not to get in his way. Is that what he had meant?

More important than what he might say is what he might do. I couldn't even let myself think about that because if I did I wouldn't be able to act and do what I had to do. I started running again. I just had to hope that Nick had found Vladimir and Mr. McCurdy and had convinced them to come and that they'd be there soon. That was assuming Nick had even found them. What if they weren't at the farmhouse anymore? They could be anywhere, including here. Maybe they were close, within earshot of me right here.

"Vladimir!" I yelled as loud as my lungs would

allow with the oxygen that wasn't driving my legs. "Mr. McCurdy! Vladimir!"

It wasn't that much farther now. It was just up ahead, just around the barn and — I was grabbed from behind, a hand was clamped over my mouth, and I was lifted right off the ground!

Chapter 11

When I realized it was Vladimir who was holding me, I felt my whole body melt in relief. He smiled, put me down, and removed his hand from my mouth.

"Vladimir, I'm so glad to —"

He clamped his hand back over my mouth. *"Shhhhhhh!"* he hissed. "Keep voice quiet." He removed his hand again.

"But you don't understand!"

"Shhhhhh!" he hissed louder, little bits of saliva hitting my face.

"That man," I whispered, "from the Armstrongs' … that bad man who wanted to buy Kushna."

"He here," Vladimir said.

"Nick told you?"

Vladimir shook his head. "Vladimir know. Man talking to Anthony now."

"But if you know that, why aren't you trying to stop him?"

"No want stop."

I felt a wave of nausea. Between the running, the

confusion, the fear of that man being here, and the shock of Vladimir grabbing me, I felt as if I was going to throw up. "But ... but ... but we have to stop them. He and Anthony are doing business. They've reached an agreement. I saw them shaking hands."

"That good news," Vladimir said.

"How can that be good news?" Now my head started spinning as much as my stomach. This could only mean one thing — Vladimir was part of the deal! Vladimir was working with Anthony to sell the tiger!

I heard footsteps behind me and turned. It was Nick and Mr. McCurdy. They were here! They could help me! They saw us, as well, and slowed to a walk. That was good. Mr. McCurdy had been barrelling along at a pace much too fast for his little old legs. Then Mr. McCurdy waved. There was a smile on his face — a smile I was going to remove when I told him Vladimir wasn't the person we'd thought he was. How could we all be so wrong about him?

"Thank goodness you caught her in time," Mr. McCurdy said before I could say anything.

"I have to talk to you," I said. "I have to explain things. I have to — what do you mean, *caught me*?"

"Before you went down there," Mr. McCurdy said. "It could have stopped everything from happening."

"But we want to stop things!" I cried. "You don't understand!"

"I do understand. Nick told me what you think and you're right. He's the man from the Armstrong place, the one who wanted to buy and butcher Kushna."

"Thank goodness you understand." I felt a wave of relief wash over me.

"And that's why we have to stay here and not interfere or even let him see us," Mr. McCurdy said.

"But that doesn't make any sense!"

"That's because there are things you don't know. That man doesn't just buy animals. He sells them. Anthony's negotiating to buy some animals from him. If he saw me or Vladimir, he'd take off and the deal would never be made. And if that happened, he'd probably sell the animals to somebody who might have other things in mind for them … not good things."

I let out a deep sigh. Suddenly, it all made sense. All those bad thoughts and feelings, all those *crazy* thoughts and feelings, were wrong. How could I ever — even for a second — have thought those things?

"I'm so sorry," I said. "I just didn't know. I could've ruined everything." I felt myself on the verge of tears. I blinked hard to hold them inside. This was embarrassing enough already without me starting to blubber.

"There, there … no harm was done," Mr. McCurdy said as he put a hand on my shoulder.

"No cry, big girl Sarah. If you cry, make Vladimir sad and Vladimir might cry."

"I don't want you crying, either!" Mr. McCurdy barked. "You're too big to be bawling!" He looked at me. "We all know you were just doing what you thought was —"

"What was that all about?" Anthony yelled as he came charging around the corner of the barn. He sounded and looked angry — no, not angry, furious. I recoiled from him and toward Mr. McCurdy.

"Sarah was just —"

"Sarah almost made this whole deal blow up in my

face!" he shouted, cutting off Mr. McCurdy.

"There was no harm. He didn't see anybody or —"

"But he *heard* her screeching. I convinced him it was just some kid visiting the farm who was screaming, but I know it unnerved him."

"Is he gone?" Mr. McCurdy asked.

"For now. He'll be back tomorrow with the animals. At least I hope he will if Sarah hasn't destroyed the deal."

The tears I'd been fighting exploded out of my eyes, and I began sobbing.

"Enough!" Mr. McCurdy yelled. "She said she was sorry and —"

"Sorry isn't good enough!" Anthony bellowed.

"You better stop cutting me off or you'll be the one who's sorry!" Mr. McCurdy snapped.

"Sorry good enough for Vladimir," the big Russian said. He stepped forward, putting himself between me and Anthony. "And if sorry not good enough for Anthony, Vladimir make Anthony feel real sorry himself."

Vladimir took a step toward Anthony. Unbelievably, Anthony didn't retreat from the oncoming giant but stepped forward himself until they were practically chest to chest! This was going from bad to worse to awful.

"Stop, please!" I pleaded as I squeezed myself into the little space between them. Neither flinched nor budged. If either moved even slightly forward, I'd be crushed.

"The girl's right," Mr. McCurdy said. He moved between them, as well, and put a hand on both men. "Now back off before I have to lay a beating on the two of you at once!"

A small smile began to grow on Vladimir's face, and a smirk evolved on Anthony's. I think the smirk was the closest thing he had to a smile. Both men appeared to deflate as their shoulders sagged and they stepped farther apart.

"Now let's all go up the farmhouse, have a coffee, and talk this one out," Mr. McCurdy suggested.

"This isn't good," Nick said.

"What isn't good?" I asked anxiously.

"They've stopped yelling."

"How is that not good?"

"When they were yelling, I could hear some of what they were saying," Nick said. "Now I can't hear anything."

"You shouldn't be trying to hear them at all," I scolded.

"Why not? It's us they're talking about … well, at least it's *you* they're talking about."

An involuntary shudder went through me. My grandmother used to say that somebody was "walking on her grave" when that happened to her. I certainly felt as if I were dead, or wanted to be dead. I wasn't used to being in trouble. I always worked so hard at doing the right thing.

Casually, I strolled across the kitchen until I was standing practically on top of my brother. Vladimir, Mr. McCurdy, and Anthony were down the hall behind a closed door in the bedroom that had been converted to an office for Tiger Town's business.

"I don't hear anything," I said.

"That's what I told you. They've stopped shouting."

"What were they saying before they stopped?" I asked.

"I thought it was wrong to eavesdrop."

"It is ... but I really want to know."

Nick didn't answer. His only response was a smug little expression that overtook his face.

"Please, Nick, it's important."

"Well, to be honest, I didn't hear a whole lot even when they were yelling."

"What did you hear?"

"There was talk about making sacrifices and doing what was right for the animals."

"Nobody would disagree with that."

"And then I heard the word *dangerous* and something about making sure nobody got hurt," he added.

"Thank goodness nobody did. Do you think that man had a gun?"

"Probably. At least they were afraid he might have had a weapon when we ran into him at the Armstrong place."

"Did you hear anything else?" I asked.

"I think I heard Anthony say that maybe it would be best if you didn't come around anymore."

"What?" I gasped.

"Maybe it would be best if you didn't —"

"I *heard* what you said. I just couldn't *believe* it."

"But don't worry. Mr. McCurdy told him there was no way that was going to happen and then Vladimir started roaring in agreement."

I felt relieved and then guilty. How could I ever have doubted Vladimir even for a second?

"You look like you were worried," Nick said.

"I was."

"Did you really think there was any chance Mr. McCurdy would ever stop you from coming to the farm?" Nick asked.

I shook my head. "I guess he wouldn't."

"You know how he feels about you, about both of us. It's the same way we feel about him."

"I know," I said. "I was just worried, that's all."

"There's nothing to be worried about. Take the word of somebody far more experienced in the art of being in trouble. In a few minutes they'll come out and give a little lecture. You have to nod a lot, sound genuinely sorry —"

"I *am* genuinely sorry."

"Excellent!" Nick said in praise. "Sound *just* like that. Even better if you can add a few tears to the mix. That would be perfect."

I was still working at fighting back more tears, but maybe I should stop. Even contemplating crying to manipulate Mr. McCurdy and Vladimir made me feel guilty. But who knows? It might help and I was desperate.

"I really have to hand it to you, Sarah," Nick said. "You don't screw up very often, but when you do, you really do it in a big way."

"Thanks for pointing that out."

"That's all part of the job of being a little brother. That and annoying you whenever possible."

"If that's the job, you're doing just great."

"Thank you."

I turned around at the sound of the door opening. There was a flash of colour as Polly flew through the opening, down the hall, and into the kitchen.

"Stupid girl!" she squawked. "Stupid girl!"

I wanted to say something back, but what was the point in arguing about something that was so obviously true?

Chapter 12

I dragged myself down the stairs of my school. It had been a long, tiring day of classes after a long, sleepless night. It would be good to get home. Maybe I could have a little nap before I started to make dinner. Then, after dinner, Nick and I would go over to see Mr. McCurdy and Vladimir. I was so grateful that I was still *allowed* to go over — what an awful thought it had been that I might not be able to go over there anymore. I didn't even know why I was still thinking about it. The trouble was over.

It was true that with all the help at Tiger Town there was less need for me and Nick, but we were still needed. Mr. McCurdy said that I was the expert on the kangaroos, and it was neat for me to know things that nobody else did. My little joeys were getting bigger all the time. It was so wonderful to see them —

A loud, jarring car horn startled me, and I spun around. It was Mr. McCurdy! He was sitting in the front seat of his big old convertible. Standing in the back seat, waving, was Calvin.

"Sarah!" Mr. McCurdy yelled.

Waving back, I realized that every eye that wasn't on him was now on me. It wasn't as if people didn't know we were close, but I suddenly felt embarrassed. What I should have been more concerned about was why Mr. McCurdy was here. Was something wrong?

I hurried my pace, wanting to get there quickly while trying to ignore the reactions I knew were going on around me. As I got close to the car — and Calvin — I wondered what people would say, how they'd react, if the chimp decided he'd forgiven me and greeted me with a big kiss. Not good. Not good at all.

"Come on, Sarah, get a move on!"

I stopped beside the passenger door. Calvin appeared to be ignoring me and was looking in the other direction, or maybe he was just fascinated by all the people milling around us.

"Get in," Mr. McCurdy said. "We have problems."

"What sort of problems?"

"Big problems. Get in and I'll explain."

I opened the door and climbed in, praying that Calvin was still too preoccupied to greet me more formally.

"Where's Nick?" Mr. McCurdy asked.

"He's got basketball practice after school."

"Too bad. I was hoping to drive you both."

"Drive us? That would be great. Can we go now?" I asked, not wanting to remain the centre of everybody's attention any longer than I had to.

"Sure." Mr. McCurdy reached into the pocket of his shirt and pulled out his driving glasses. They were pink rhinestone women's cat's-eye glasses, which just about completed the picture. He turned the key, and the engine began grinding and whining, but it didn't catch.

Oh, dear God, please let it start. Please don't leave me stranded in this convertible with a chimp, surrounded by just about everybody from my school. I closed my eyes and kept praying. Then I heard the engine start!

"Amen," I said softly, opening my eyes as the gears ground noisily and we moved forward. I slumped down in the seat to disappear at least a little bit.

"You mentioned a problem," I said.

"Big problem," Mr. McCurdy said.

"What sort of problem?"

"We got in some new animals this morning."

"Did one of them escape?" I asked, thinking about Buddha.

"No, none of 'em, though it would've been better if some of 'em never arrived. We got a European lynx, a couple of buffalo, and a dozen more parrots. It's the parrots that are the problem."

"That's a lot of new parrots, but you can put them in the same enclosure for a while until you build a bigger one," I suggested.

"It's not the enclosure that's the problem. You probably don't know, but parrots can carry diseases — infectious diseases."

"Polly … is Polly okay?"

"Polly's never around the other parrots. Polly doesn't even *like* parrots. But that was sweet of you to be worried. Some of these diseases are harmless to parrots. They only hurt people."

"People? You mean *you* could get infected?"

"I was infected. Over forty years ago. Got sick as a

dog for a month, but I recovered. Other people aren't that lucky."

"Then you have to stay away from those parrots," I said. "You don't want to catch it again."

"That's the thing. Once you've had it you can't get it again. Your body builds up these things, these, um … I forget what you call 'em …"

"Antibodies," I said. "We've been studying them in health class. It's like once you get measles you can't get it a second time."

"Exactly. So I'm safe."

"What about Vladimir?" I asked.

"Same thing. Had it in Russia over ten years ago, so he's safe, too."

"And Anthony?" I didn't know why I was even asking. As far as I was concerned, I didn't care if he caught hoof-and-mouth disease. Then I felt bad for feeling that way.

"Funniest thing. Anthony thinks he had a mild case himself. But just to be safe he's going to stay completely away from the parrots. Same as Bob and Doug — they're going to stay clear away from that area of Tiger Town."

"That's probably smart to be safe like that," I said.

"I'm glad you agree because that's why I picked you up. I had to tell you and Nick that you can't come over to the farm."

"We can't?"

"Nobody can. The health department has put us under quarantine. No visitors, no volunteers, no nobody can come to Tiger Town."

"What if we stayed away from the parrots?" I suggested. "We could stay clear on the other side of the farm."

"Can't do that, Sarah. Can't break the law and can't risk anything happening to either you or Nick. You know how much I care about the two of you."

Mr. McCurdy saying that made me feel a little bit better. "How long do we have to stay away?"

"Could be as little as three weeks."

"Or as long as?"

"Up to six or eight weeks," Mr. McCurdy said.

"Eight weeks! That's practically forever."

"We'll hope for less, but there's nothing we can do," he said.

"But what about Kanga and Roo? Who will take care of them?"

"We'll do our best. If we have any questions, we know you're just a phone call away. Don't you trust me to take care of them?"

"Of course I do. It's just that it's such a long time to be away from them, and Laura and Calvin and Vladimir … and you."

He smiled. "The animals have to stay on the farm, but you can count on me and Vladimir coming over to visit a couple of times. It isn't just you who'll miss us."

"That would be nice. I'll make you both a really special, big dinner."

"Make us a few big dinners and you'll see us more than a couple of times. Now I need you to do me a big favour."

"Anything."

"As soon as I drop you home, I need you to get on the phone and start calling people, all the volunteers we have, and tell 'em they can't come around until they hear from us again."

“I can do that.” I paused. “By the way, in case somebody asks, what’s the name of this disease?”

“It’s some big fancy word I have trouble saying. Must be Latin or Greek or something. Just tell ’em to stay away.”

“I’ll do that as soon as I get home, but there’s one thing I need to know. What you’re telling me … it’s true, right?”

“You think I’m lying?” Mr. McCurdy asked. He sounded upset.

“Not lying. Just sort of protecting me. You’re not really in any danger, are you? You can’t get the disease, right?”

“Sarah, you have my word on that. Believe me, there’s absolutely no chance I can get that disease.”

That made me feel a lot better. “That’s all I needed to know.”

I settled back in my seat. It wouldn’t be great, but it would be okay eventually. Funny, though, just yesterday Anthony wanted me to stay away from the farm, and now I couldn’t go there — nobody could. What an odd coincidence.

Chapter 13

"Moping around the house isn't going to make the time pass any quicker," my mother said.

"It won't make it pass any slower, either," I shot back. It couldn't be any slower than it seemed. It had only been five days. An incredibly slow five days.

"You have to go back to doing what you did before you spent time at the farm with Mr. McCurdy and his animals."

"The things I used to do involved hanging around with my friends, the friends I'd had since I was in kindergarten, the friends I left behind when we moved here."

"That's not fair, Sarah. We've lived here for almost a year and a half. Besides, it isn't as if you don't have friends here."

"I have friends," I admitted, though it seemed as if a lot of those friendships involved being at Tiger Town. "But maybe I do want to just mope around."

"Far be it from me to tell you what to do. After all, I'm only your mother."

I bit my tongue before I said anything I'd regret,

something that was going to get harder the longer I spent time at home. "Does Martin know about the quarantine?" I asked.

"He's the chief of police. He knows everything. Matter of fact, he told me I had to make certain you and Nick don't go anywhere near Tiger Town until the quarantine's lifted. He said it was very, very important and was quite insistent. I had no idea parrots could carry anything that potentially dangerous to humans."

"Neither did I," I said. "I tried to get more information off the Internet, but I couldn't find anything."

"Nothing?"

"Not a thing about any illness that could be fatal to humans."

"That's surprising," my mother said. "You'd figure that would be on there for sure."

"It would be better if I knew the name of the disease."

"That would help. I thought Mr. McCurdy promised he'd get you the name of the disease. Didn't you ask him that when he and Vladimir were over for dinner?"

"I did. He said he'd talk to Anthony and get the name because he couldn't remember it since it was such a big word."

"But he still hasn't told you the name?" my mother asked.

"Nope."

"That's understandable, I guess. He does have a lot on his mind."

"So do I."

"The only thing that should be on your mind is school."

"What about school?" I asked.

"I've been meaning to mention it to you. There's been a drop in your grades this term."

"I have an eighty-nine average."

"And it was ninety-three last year."

"It's still pretty good. If Nick got an eighty-nine average on his report card, you'd buy him a pony."

"If Nick got an eighty-nine average, I'd get him a blood test so I could see what drugs he was taking that were making him so smart."

I burst out laughing.

My mother looked a little sheepish, as if she knew she'd said something she really shouldn't have. "Please don't tell Nick I said that. I just know how well you can do."

"I am doing well."

"You could do better. In this day and age it's important for a woman to be self-sufficient, to be able to support herself, because there are no guarantees she's always going to have a husband to —"

"Don't worry about me getting divorced, because it isn't going to happen."

"Don't be so certain," my mother said. "I never dreamed it would happen to me, either."

"With me it's practically a guarantee. If you don't ever get married, you can't ever get divorced."

"Sarah, just because your father and I couldn't make our marriage work is no reason for you to feel you couldn't have a successful marriage."

"This has nothing to do with that. Nothing. Not everything is about your divorce. I just might have other things I want to do with my life, and a marriage might just get in the way."

"Don't rule out marriage," she said. "I haven't."

I knew what she was implying. She and Martin had gotten awfully close, awfully quick. Maybe too close and too quick.

"All I'm saying is —"

"I know exactly what you're saying!" I snapped. "But just because I know doesn't mean I think you're right."

My mother didn't answer. She was hurt. I wanted to say something, but I didn't know what exactly. "I think I'll go for a walk," I finally murmured.

"That sounds like a good idea," my mother said. "Do you want some company?"

"I guess that would be okay … I guess."

"It sounds as if you'd rather be alone but are being too polite to say it."

I nodded. "Sometimes I just like to be alone with my thoughts."

"And that's okay. Most people aren't comfortable being on their own." She stood up, walked over, and placed a hand on each of my shoulders. "Sarah, you're very special, and maybe I don't say that enough."

"Thanks, Mom."

"You're welcome. I know this growing-up stuff isn't easy sometimes. Not for you and not for me. We'll all keep learning. Part of what I have to keep reminding myself is that you're not a little girl anymore." She leaned down and kissed me on the forehead.

I could feel fall beginning to give way to winter. The air was crisp and cool and traced a path down into my lungs as I breathed in. The temperature was dropping as quickly as the sun was falling toward the horizon. It was only seven-thirty and it would be dark soon. I wanted to get safely home before that happened.

I turned off the road and onto a path that ran along the fence separating our land from Mr. McCurdy's. This route was rougher, but it was a lot shorter. The last thing I wanted was to be out here alone in the dark.

I walked along the stone fence. Actually, it was more like a long line of rocks that had, over the past hundred years, been pulled out of the fields of both properties and piled up as a fence. I had to fight the urge to climb over the divide and walk on the other side — on Mr. McCurdy's property. In one way it would have felt good just to have his soil under my shoes. On the other hand, I wasn't supposed to be there and I always tried to keep my word. What if somebody saw me or —

"Hi, Sarah."

I shrieked, jumped into the air, and spun around. Frantically, I looked around. There was nobody there!

"Up here."

I still didn't see anybody, but I knew the voice. It was Nick's. "Up where?"

"Here," he called out.

I followed his voice and then caught sight of movement in the limbs of a tree. He was sitting high in the branches, his feet dangling down. "What are you doing up there?"

"Just sitting and watching."

"Watching what?"

"The house."

"You can see our house from here?"

"Not our house. Mr. McCurdy's house."

"You're joking."

"Nope. Why else do you think I'd be sitting up here?"

"I can hardly ever figure out why you do anything," I said.

"Come on up here and see the house for yourself."

I didn't like heights and I certainly didn't go around climbing trees anymore, but I did want to see the house, even from a distance.

Glancing up at the branches, I tried to map a route to where Nick sat among the very top limbs. It didn't look that hard. I reached up and grabbed the lowest limb, pulling myself up until I could throw my leg over. Slowly, testing each branch before I put my full weight on it, I worked my way up the tree until I was just below Nick.

"That was certainly interesting," Nick said. "It was sort of like watching a slow-motion replay."

"Better safe than sorry," I said.

"I don't know. The way you climb actually *is* sorry."

"Excuse me if I'm not a monkey."

"Or a chimpanzee," Nick said. "But I wish you were. Do you miss Calvin as much as I do?"

"If he was here, *I'd* kiss *him*."

Nick burst into laughter, teetered, and almost toppled over before he grabbed the branch to steady himself.

"Be careful."

"I am being careful. Even if I fell, it isn't that far down. I couldn't get hurt very much." He glanced down. "Well, not real bad."

"So where's the house?" I asked.

"You have to look through the gap between the two big branches."

I pushed myself up and peered through the opening. I didn't see anything … except for the lane leading to Tiger Town.

"Now if you see the driveway you can follow it along to the right until —"

"I see it!" I cried. "I can see the front door! And over to the side I can see part of the barn and a little bit of Peanuts' pen."

"Can you see Peanuts?"

I tried to focus on that little section of his pen poking around the side of the barn. He wasn't —

"Peanuts!" Nick screamed, practically shocking and shaking me out of the tree. "Peanuts!" Nick yelled again.

"What are you doing?"

"Calling my elephant."

"He can't hear you from here. The barn's a long, long way off. All you did was practically scare me out of the tree."

"Did you hear that?" Nick asked.

"Hear what?"

"Shhhhhhh!"

There was a low, long, rumbling roar.

"Hear him? And look!" Nick said, pointing into the distance.

I stared at the barn again. Peanuts was in the corner of the pen that I could see, gazing in our direction, his trunk in the air. Then I heard the elephant call out again.

"Elephants have big ears and big lungs," Nick said. "He heard me yell his name and then he called back. Isn't he a good elephant?"

"The best one I ever met. I just wish I could

communicate with Kanga and Roo the same way."

"You must really miss them," Nick said.

I was surprised. Nick usually didn't show much sensitivity.

"It's hard being away from Peanuts," Nick said. "It's hard being away from things that are important to you."

I wondered if he was really talking about our father, but I knew I couldn't say that. "It's hard. But you have to figure that even if you're not around that they still think about you and miss you, too."

"I guess so," Nick said.

We sat in the tree, not talking, just watching the farmhouse. Actually, I wondered again if Nick was focused farther away from there — maybe thinking about our father on the other side of the country. As we sat there silently, the sun continued to sink lower until it was a red ball on the edge of the horizon.

"We should get down and go home before it gets any darker," I suggested.

"You're right. Let's climb down before — look, there are headlights coming down the lane!"

There, along the lane of Mr. McCurdy's farm, was a pair of headlights.

"Do you think it's Mr. McCurdy?" Nick asked.

"Could be or — there's a second set of lights!"

"And a third!" Nick called out.

"That's one more vehicle than the farm has."

"I can't even see if it's a truck or a car," Nick said.

"It doesn't matter. Whoever it is they shouldn't be there, anyway."

"It could be somebody else who's already had the disease, too," Nick said.

"Could be," I agreed. "Don't you think it's strange, though, that the only three people at the farm have all had the disease?"

"Coincidences happen."

"That's a *big* coincidence."

"Even big coincidences happen," Nick said. "Let's go home."

Chapter 14

I jumped from page to page, moving the mouse and clicking on the websites I'd marked. I'd spent hours — no, I'd spent *days* — searching, reading, marking, studying, researching. I'd been through the pages, following the links as if they were stones along the Yellow Brick Road, hoping they'd finally lead me to Oz. Instead they'd just spun me around and around as if I were Dorothy inside the twister.

I was at the point where I was an expert on parrots. I was a walking, talking encyclopedia on parrots. Then again, an encyclopedia of parrots should probably talk and walk and even fly. I knew about the different species, habitat, and every aspect of their life cycles. I knew everything. Especially everything about illnesses and diseases. I knew the most common ailments and sicknesses and the treatments. I knew diseases that parrots got from people and diseases people got from parrots. The worst of the latter could cause people to get really sick, even suffer temporary paralysis, but there was nothing that could kill somebody, nothing you could catch from kilometres away, nothing like the thing that was supposed to be in Tiger Town.

"This is useless!" I yelled, slamming my hand against the tabletop.

"No luck, huh?"

I looked over my shoulder. It was Nick.

"Lots of luck," I said. "All bad."

"Can't find anything about the disease?" he asked.

"Nothing. But why should something turn up now? I've been through this information a dozen times."

"You shouldn't exaggerate."

"I'm not. That was my twelfth time through. I kept thinking I'd find something that I missed if I just kept on looking."

"You were just wasting your time," Nick said.

"And what was it you were doing with your time?"

"I was sitting in a tree."

"Again? You've spent a lot of time in that tree the past week. More than I've spent in front of this computer."

"About the same," he said. "But I wasn't wasting my time."

"How do you figure that sitting in a tree is a better use of time than surfing the Web?"

"I knew there was a chance I might find something," he said.

"There was a chance I could find something, too, you know."

"No, there wasn't. You can't find something that doesn't exist."

"What do you mean?"

Nick didn't answer right away. "If I tell you, you might think I have a loose screw."

"I've always thought you had a *lot* of loose screws, so this won't make any difference. Just tell me."

He seemed hesitant to answer, but I knew if I waited him out he'd start talking. Nick hated silence.

"Three weeks ago, when this all started, I was positive everything we were being told was the truth," he finally said. "Last week I was pretty sure. Now I'm positive most of what we've been told isn't true."

"You don't think there's a disease?"

"If there was, you'd have found it on the Net. Besides, if there was a quarantine, how come people are coming and going at the farm?"

"You mean that extra set of headlights we saw when we were sitting in the tree?"

"I mean those and all the other cars and trucks I've seen coming and going over the past few days. I've spotted eleven vehicles."

"That many?"

He nodded. "And those are just the ones I've seen. I've been in the tree a lot, but not all the time. If I saw that many, think of how many I must have missed."

He was right.

"Why would so many vehicles be coming and going?" Nick asked.

"Maybe they didn't know the place was quarantined and drove in without knowing."

"The big yellow quarantine sign posted at the driveway is hard to miss," Nick said.

"There's a sign?"

"Big and yellow and right there by the driveway."

"When did you see it?" I asked.

"Yesterday. I took a stroll past the entrance."

"Still, maybe some people missed the sign … just didn't see it."

"Even if they did miss the sign, why weren't they turned back when they arrived instead of staying for hours?"

"They stayed?"

"Some of them. For hours."

"That is strange," I agreed.

"And there's one more thing," Nick said. "It's about Anthony."

"What about him?"

"You'll think I'm strange for even thinking this," Nick said.

"Nick, I think we've already established that I've always thought you were strange. Spit it out."

"Don't get mad at me because of what I'm going to say."

"I'm getting mad at you for what you're *not* saying."

"Fine. Do you know who Anthony reminds me of?"

"You better not say me, or I really am going to be mad at you," I said.

"Actually … he does … a bit. But I was thinking that he really reminds me of Dad."

"Dad? He reminds you of our father? I don't see that at all."

"Not like Dad was before, but what he was like the last few months before he left," Nick explained.

"Go on."

"You know how he was really, really friendly. Too friendly. And it was like he knew something was going to happen, something bad — the separation — but he was trying to keep it from us."

"I remember."

"And that's what Anthony's like. He was always real friendly, at least to me, but he was hiding something."

"He was trying to hide the fact that he was a jerk," I said.

"I didn't say he was a jerk, just that he was hiding something from us."

"Doesn't that make him a jerk?" I asked.

"Not necessarily," Nick said. "Dad was trying to hide the marriage problems from us to protect us."

"And he did a great job of that!" I snapped.

"He tried."

"He tried and failed. Besides, when somebody's trying to hide something, it isn't something good."

"Probably not."

"Do you think he's fooling Vladimir and Mr. McCurdy, too?" I asked.

"I hope he is."

"Why would you hope that?"

"Because if he isn't fooling them, then they're in on his plan, too."

"What plan?" I asked.

"Well, there are some other things I didn't mention to you."

"What sort of things?"

"Things like I saw that truck come back ... the truck that man drove ... the man who tried to buy Kushna."

"They might have been buying more animals from him," I suggested.

"That wouldn't explain why there are empty cages now."

"There are empty — how would you know that? You can't see the enclosures from that tree."

"Not from *that* tree."

"And just what other tree were you in?" I asked.

"Before I answer, can I ask you a question?"

"Are you trying to worm your way out of being in trouble, or is this a legitimate question?"

"Both."

I shrugged. "Go ahead."

"If we were supposed to stay away because of some disease but there really isn't such a disease, is it wrong for me to go on Mr. McCurdy's property?"

I knew what he was getting at. "How far onto his property did you go?"

"You know that little stand of trees by the pond beside the barn?"

"You went that close?"

"I had to get that close or I couldn't see what I needed to see," Nick explained.

"And?"

"I saw empty cages. Kanga and Roo's pen was empty."

"Are you … are you sure? Maybe you couldn't see them in there."

"Sarah, I was practically right there. I could see the whole pen, and they weren't in it. Do you think they brought them back inside again?"

"Why would they do that?" I asked. The two kangaroos had been moved outdoors three weeks ago — they were big and strong enough that they didn't need to live inside anymore.

"Maybe they just needed extra attention," Nick said.

"Maybe they were sad because you weren't around."

"That could be it," I agreed — more hoping and wishing than really believing.

"If they miss you as much as you miss them, then that could be it," Nick said. "It could be other things, too."

"What sort of other things?"

"Look, I have some ideas about this whole business. That doesn't mean they're right ideas, but I really, really have been thinking about things, trying to figure it all out."

"And?"

"And I don't know how you do it all the time — thinking, I mean. I've been thinking about it so much it's made my brain go numb."

"Fine, whatever," I said. "Just tell me what you've been thinking."

"I'll tell you, but I don't really want to. I was just wondering. Do you think it's possible the kangaroos aren't in their pen because they've been sold?"

"No," I said, shaking my head vigorously. "No way they've been sold. There's no way Anthony could get away with that without Vladimir and Mr. McCurdy knowing. It isn't like there are dozens of kangaroos around."

"That's the other part I've been thinking about," Nick said. "What if … what if Mr. McCurdy and Vladimir are part of it."

"Part of what?"

"Part of selling off the animals. What if it isn't just Anthony but all three of them working together?"

"You can't be serious," I said. "There's no way they'd ever do that. They'd never do anything to harm any of their animals."

"They might. You remember when I was listening in on their argument about you? I heard them saying things about *sacrifice*, and *making choices*, and sometimes you have to make the *hard* decisions. What if they weren't talking about you and me being in Tiger Town, but about selling off some of the animals?"

"That's crazy," I said. "Crazy!"

"Is it? If selling one tiger could let them get enough money to save a dozen tigers, don't you think they'd at least consider it?"

"They'd never ... would they?" I tried to think things through. "I just don't know."

"I don't know, either," Nick said. "Maybe I'm just letting my imagination run away."

"Maybe. Maybe not. There's only one way we can know for sure. We have to go over and investigate."

"It's not that easy, Sarah, believe me."

"Easy or not we have to do it."

"I almost got caught. They almost saw me."

"We're not going to get caught and nobody's going to see us," I said. "It's going to be way too dark to be seen."

"You mean?"

I nodded. "Tonight. When Mom's asleep and everybody at the farm is asleep. Then we go."

Chapter 15

As silently as possible, I closed the kitchen door behind us. It made a slight noise, but there was no way that Mom, all the way upstairs in her bedroom soundly asleep, could have heard it. Nick and I started off, trying to keep the sound of our footfalls quiet, as well. We moved quickly, finally stopping and glancing back as we reached the row of trees and bushes that formed a windbreak to the north of our house.

"It's awfully bright out here," Nick said.

Now that he'd mentioned it I realized he was right. It was a cloudless evening, and a big, bright, full moon dominated a sky filled with thousands and thousands of stars. It was all so beautiful. I wished I could sit and watch the heavens. That would definitely be safer than what we were going to do.

"I guess we won't be needing the flashlights," Nick said.

"That's not good."

"How can that not be good?"

"Maybe we can see where we're walking," I said,

"but other people can see us walking more easily."

"What other people? It's the middle of the night and everybody — even the few people there are — are all asleep."

"We hope they are, but what about all those cameras?" I reminded him. "They'll be able to see us."

"That's not a problem. Just because the cameras pick us up and we're shown on the monitors doesn't mean anybody's there to see the monitors."

"I guess that makes sense, but it still creeps me out to think that people could be watching us and we wouldn't even know it."

"Sarah, believe me, if somebody's watching us sneak around in the middle of the night when we're not supposed to be there to begin with, then we'll know they're watching us real quick."

That was logical, but it didn't exactly give me the reassurance I was looking for. "I still don't know why Anthony had all those cameras installed."

"To watch the animals," Nick said.

"If that was why, then how come most of the cameras seem to be aimed at the paths between the cages rather than at the animals?"

"They look at both because the danger to the animals would probably be coming along the paths. Besides, why else would the cameras have been installed?"

It was a good question, but I didn't have a good answer. All I had was that uneasy feeling in the pit of my stomach and the back of my head. It was as if those cameras were just like Anthony himself — always watching everybody and everything. But why?

I had the same feeling about those cameras that I

had about anything to do with Anthony. There were too many questions, too many things that didn't make sense about him, but what I did know was that he hadn't been telling us the truth about lots of things. Maybe I wasn't a fantastic liar, but he didn't seem to be that great at it, either.

Nick climbed onto the rock-pile fence that marked the property line. He dropped down the other side, and I heard a couple of loose rocks shift underneath him. I followed, stopping at the very top, the spot dividing the two properties, the place that separated where I *should* be from where I *shouldn't* be. Actually, I shouldn't be standing right here in the middle of the night, either. I should have been in my bed asleep. I guess I was already wrong; it was just a question of how wrong I was going to become. It wasn't too late. We could still return home, get back into bed, and nobody would know any different.

"Sarah!" Nick called out. "You should get down. You can probably be seen in the next town!"

I scrambled off the rocks and onto Mr. McCurdy's property. Somehow that meant the decision was made. Standing at the top of the fence, I could have gone either way. Now there was only one direction.

Without exchanging a word Nick took the lead. We'd talked about him taking us in the same way he'd gone in yesterday. Now we cut into a stand of trees that ran between two fields. Instantly, it became darker as the branches overhead blocked out the moonlight. We had to slow down, but that was fine because I felt more protected, safer from prying eyes or cameras, thinking that maybe there weren't any cameras in the trees.

I tried to recall the one time I'd been in the control room, looking at all the monitors. There were lots of cameras, dozens and dozens, but they were all hidden in the lights that stood on the paths. That meant there were none in the trees, none in the fields, and none down behind the barn — places where visitors to the farm weren't allowed to go. At least that made some sense.

The small stand of trees ended. Up ahead I could clearly make out the barn, dark and towering, and the pond — the moon reflecting brightly off the water. Just beyond the barn were the pens — rows upon rows of them. There were more pens now than there had been three weeks ago. Why hadn't Nick mentioned that? Maybe that was why some of the pens were empty. Perhaps that was why Kango and Roo weren't in their pen, because they now had a different one. If that was the case, we didn't even need to be here and we could just return home.

Then I realized that wasn't the only reason we were here. Fear for the safety of my kangaroos had been the final straw, but there was a whole haystack full of reasons we needed to be here.

"We have to avoid the paths," I whispered to Nick.

"Why?"

I stared at him as if he were crazy. "The cameras, remember?"

He shot back a look that said I was crazy, too. "Nobody's watching them, remember?"

"I don't care. We should still stay out of the light as much as we can."

The lights that held the hidden cameras stretched out along the paths. Each one cast a little halo of illumination.

"There are no lights on in the house," Nick said.

I gazed past the pens to the darkened farmhouse. Somehow I'd forgotten about it being right there — about them being right there. Thank goodness it was dark. Nobody was awake.

"First thing I want to do is see Peanuts," Nick said.

"The *last* thing we'll do is see Peanuts, and only if we have time. We're not here for a visit. We're here to investigate. We'll start with the pens — and speaking of pens, why didn't you tell me there were new ones?"

"Didn't I mention that?"

I shook my head. "I think I would've remembered."

"I guess I just forgot because so much is happening."

"I want to see the new pens first. I want to see what new animals are in them. There might be a clue."

"I guess that makes sense," Nick agreed.

Thank goodness Nick didn't ask what sort of clue, because I didn't have any idea. Part of wanting to go to the new cages was to see if Kanga and Roo were there. I wanted to see them as much as Nick wanted to see Peanuts. Actually, I needed to see my roos. At least Nick knew Peanuts was still here, though I hadn't seen him in the outside part of his enclosure. But that just meant he was inside the barn.

Nick took a route between two of the cages. On one side there was a jaguar and on the other a leopard. At least that's what those pens had held three weeks ago. I caught a glint of glowing golden eyes — jaguar eyes. They disappeared and then reappeared as the big cat blinked. As I watched the eyes watching me, they started to move forward, gliding on silent feline feet until the cat itself materialized — powerful, beautiful, deadly. I knew what the cat was doing. It was stalking me. It was hoping that somehow the fence it knew was there would suddenly vanish. Even though I could see the fence and knew I was safe, I didn't feel secure. I angled slightly away, making sure I didn't get too close to the fence on the other side and the cat it held.

Suddenly, the silence was shattered by the roar of a lion. I froze on the spot, and the hair on the back of my neck stood straight up. He roared again. Then from another direction a leopard snarled, the wolves began howling, and —

"Lights!" Nick hissed. "A light just came on at the house."

My head spun around. There was a light on in one of the lower windows. The noise had woken somebody up. Then a second light flicked on. More than one person was awake now. Of course, just because they were awake didn't mean they'd come out to investigate. The animals made noises all the time. The light outside the back door was switched on, and the door popped open — it was Anthony!

I dropped flat to the ground, and Nick did the same.

"We have to get out of here," I whispered, starting to crawl back the way we'd come. As long as we stayed low and didn't make any noise, we could get to those trees and from there we could sprint home. Slithering forward, I kept peeking up at Anthony. He was standing there, still as a statue, staring out into the night, trying to see what had disturbed the animals. Not that he cared about them. He was just worried that if something happened it could cost him some money.

If he continued to stand there, maybe he'd eventually

go back inside. If he did that, we could continue looking around. I hardly believed I was brave enough even to think that thought, but I didn't want to leave unless the truth left with me. I stopped in my tracks. We'd just wait him out and — Nick bumped into my butt, knocking me forward onto my face.

"Why did you stop?" Nick whispered.

"If we stay, maybe Anthony will go back into —" I broke off as Anthony began walking toward the enclosures. Then he started jogging. He was coming in our direction. Had he seen us? I had to fight the urge to jump up and run. We had to stay still. If he hadn't seen us, we were safe. If he had and we ran, he'd see us for sure. Even if we did outrun him, it wasn't as if he didn't know who we were or where we lived.

Anthony kept moving in our direction, closer and closer until he sped right by the opening.

"Where's he going?" I questioned.

"Only one place I can think of," Nick said. "The control room."

"Oh, my goodness!" I gasped.

"And in about thirty seconds he's going to be able to see all of the cameras, everywhere."

"What are we going to do?" I asked.

"We're going to run. We have thirty seconds to get away!"

Nick jumped to his feet, and I stumbled to mine. He raced full speed across the open area leading to the barn. There were no lights in that area so there were no cameras down the side of the barn. So if we could get that far before Anthony reached the control room we could make it to the fields that led to the trees that bordered our property. I put my head down and ran as fast as my legs could carry me. Nick got to the side of the barn and disappeared down the incline. I was only seconds behind him … seconds away from safety. I hit the top of the hill, then lost my footing and toppled over, tumbling down the slope and coming to a stop in a heap at the bottom.

"Sarah, are you all right?" Nick reached down and grabbed my hand, pulling me to my feet.

"I'm okay," I said, not even checking to see what I might have hurt. I knew my knees ached. "Do you think he saw us?"

"We moved pretty fast. I don't think he had time to get there, unlock the door, check the monitors, and —"

He stopped. We both heard the same thing. Footsteps were coming rapidly along the path.

"In here!" Nick said.

I hesitated, but he seized my hand and led me into the small side door opening into the stable of the barn. We staggered into the darkness, the only thing allowing us to move at all being our knowledge of the floor plan.

"Let's hide in the hay," Nick whispered.

"The hay? Where Brent lives?" Brent was Mr. McCurdy's three-metre-long Burmese python.

"Do you have a better idea?"

Any idea had to be better than that. Maybe we could go upstairs, cut around Peanuts' enclosure, and then shoot out the other way.

I heard voices — male voices — coming from outside the door we had just entered!

"Up here!" I hissed, and gestured to Nick to follow me.

Shuffling along the straw-covered floor, I spied something moving off to the side and stopped, frozen in place as I peered into the darkness, trying to see. In a cage I made out two figures. Then one of the shapes *bounded*! Both figures hopped toward the bars — it was Kanga and Roo! They were here, they were safe! I felt like yelling or laughing or … Then I heard the voice again, this time louder.

"Come on!" I said to Nick, and we started up the steep stairs that led out of the stable to the barn's main floor. I bent over and used my hands to scale the steps. Trying to move fast, I realized I wasn't doing so quietly as my feet thumped against the wooden stairs.

"In here!" I heard a voice call out. "In the barn!"

I scrambled up the remaining stairs and halted, too stunned to know which way to go or where to hide or what to do!

"Don't move!" a voice yelled. "Don't take another step! Put your hands up! Now!"

Slowly, I lifted my hands above my head. We were caught. It was over. Strangely, I was filled with a sense of relief, and that was better than the fear that had been filling my gut. I opened my mouth to say something when the whole room became filled with brilliant light. I put up my hands to shield myself from the blinding glare.

"Sarah, Nick …"

I moved my hand and saw Doug, one of the new employees Anthony had hired. Doug looked as confused as I felt frightened. He was standing by the light switch. Right behind him, in his pen, stood Peanuts.

"What are you two doing here?" he demanded.

I blinked. "We were just —"

"You really shouldn't be here. You're going to have to explain all this to Anthony." Doug had a walkie-talkie clipped to his belt. He pulled it up to his mouth. "This is Doug … I'm in the barn and I've got them … it's Sarah and Nick."

There was static and then a reply.

"Hold on to them … I'll be right there!" Anthony barked so loud I could hear him over the radio. He didn't sound happy.

"Peanuts!" Nick called out. "Are you okay, boy?" Nick began walking toward the pen.

Unbelievably, despite everything, all he wanted to do was visit his elephant. Didn't he know how much trouble we were in, what could happen to us? Actually, I didn't even know the answer to those questions.

Without warning Nick broke for the door. For a split second it looked as if he might make it when Doug jumped forward and grabbed him!

"You're not going anywhere!" Doug shouted.

"Let me go!" Nick cried. "Let me go!"

Doug had Nick firmly by the arm and was marching him away from the door when Peanuts reached his trunk over the bars of his enclosure and seized Doug. As Doug was lifted into the air, he released his grip on Nick, who fell to the floor. Doug screamed — a blood-curdling yell — as Peanuts raised him higher and higher and then tossed him. Pinwheeling through the air, arms and legs flailing, Doug landed with a thud against the wall.

Before I could even think to react — whether to flee or run to see if Doug was okay — Anthony and Bob appeared in the doorway. I stepped back as Nick picked himself up off the straw-covered floor and scampered over to my side. He hid slightly behind me as if seeking protection. Maybe we both should have jumped into the pen with Peanuts.

"What's going on here?" Anthony bellowed. "What are you doing here?" He glanced at Doug, who was sitting on the ground and rubbing his head, seemingly in pain. Anthony turned to Bob. "See if he's all right."

Switching his attention to us, Anthony stared straight at me — an angry, hard, hot glare. I felt a wave of panic and fear — stronger than I'd ever experienced in my entire life.

"You shouldn't have come here," he said. His voice was quiet. That was worse, more scary, than if he'd yelled. "I've tried everything I could think of to make you stay away, but you just keep coming back."

"We won't come back again," Nick pleaded. He sounded as if he were on the verge of tears. It was up to me to defend him … defend me.

"We want to see Mr. McCurdy or Vladimir," I demanded.

"They can't help you now," he said threateningly. "It's too late."

The fear I was experiencing suddenly jumped right off the scale. What did he mean *too late*? Too late for what?"

"There's only *one* thing left for me to do," he said ominously. "I tried to avoid this, but you don't leave me any alternative." He opened up his jacket. There, in a leather holster, was a gun!

Chapter 16

"You can't do that!" I gasped. "You can't shoot us!"

"Shoot you?" He sounded almost as confused as I felt scared.

I pointed at the gun strapped to his side.

"Nobody's going to shoot anybody," Anthony said. "What I'm going to do is tell you the truth. I guess sometimes that can work when everything else fails."

He opened his jacket farther to reveal the gun even more. Then he reached into his pocket and pulled out a wallet. Was he going to pay us to go away? If he let us go right now, I'd do it for free.

"Do you know who I am?" he asked.

"I know *what* you are!" I snapped, amazed at how I was either brave enough or stupid enough to give attitude to a guy with a gun.

"Sarah … settle down," Nick said out of the side of his mouth.

"That's okay, Nick. So, Sarah, do you really think you know what I am?"

That sickly sweet smirk filled his face. If I had gun, I'd have shot *him*.

He flipped open his wallet. There was a badge — a big silver shield — in the wallet. "My name's Anthony Mednis and I'm an agent of the United Nations, working under the mandate of international legislation to protect endangered and exotic animals."

"W-what?" I sputtered. "You're what?"

"A special agent."

"I ... I don't understand," I stammered, peering at the badge, trying to make sense of what I was seeing, what he'd just said and what had been going on here.

"You're a cop?" Nick asked.

"An *agent*," Anthony said, "a special agent working for the Wildlife Conservation Foundation under the authority of the United Nations. Myself, Bob, and Doug and —" He turned around to where Doug sat and Bob hovered over him. "Is he okay?"

"I'm okay," Doug answered weakly. "But my arm's hurt."

"It could be broken," Bob added.

"Damn!" Anthony said. "We can't have that happen. Especially not now. Get him up to the house."

Bob helped Doug to his feet. The way he was holding his arm — cradling it with the other — left no doubt he was hurt. The only question was how badly.

"You two come, too," Anthony said. "We'll sort out the rest of this up there."

Anthony followed Doug and Bob out of the barn, leaving Nick and I standing there alone. For a split second I thought we could just run away now, but I knew we couldn't do that.

"Come on," I said to Nick, and we both hurried out the door after them. We quickly caught up — Doug didn't seem to be able to move very quickly.

"It was an accident," I said to Doug.

"Peanuts didn't mean to harm anybody," Nick said. "He was just trying to defend me."

"I shouldn't have grabbed you," Doug said feebly. "I was just afraid to let you go before we talked to you … I couldn't believe how far that elephant threw me."

"You just flew!" Nick said, sounding almost enthusiastic.

"Don't you want to know why we're here?" I asked Anthony, changing the subject quickly away from Nick and Peanuts and Doug being hurt.

"I know why you're here," Anthony said. "You're here because you didn't believe the lie we made up about the place being under quarantine."

"Then there really wasn't a disease," I said.

"There are lots of diseases, but not one like the one I created to shoo everybody away."

"You lied to us," I said, stating the obvious.

"I lie to almost *everybody*. That's part of my job."

"But what about Mr. McCurdy and Vladimir?" I asked.

"Them I didn't lie to. They know everything and have from almost the beginning. At least after I found out I could trust them. Let me look after Doug before you pester me with any more questions. Let's just go inside."

"Is Mr. McCurdy in there?" I asked. "Is Vladimir in there?"

"Angus is. Vladimir's out doing something for us.

I asked Angus to stay inside until we sorted things out. I didn't want him getting shot."

"Shot?" Nick said. "You thought we might have a gun?"

"We didn't know it was you," Anthony said. "All we knew is that some of these people do carry weapons and they don't care about people any more than they care about animals."

Nick rushed ahead and opened the door to the farmhouse. I trailed after everybody, down the hall and into the kitchen.

"Sarah! Nick!" Mr. McCurdy called out. He jumped up from the kitchen table, hurried over, and wrapped an arm around both of us. It felt so good, so safe to have him there. "What are you two doing here?" he questioned.

"I guess we were the intruders," I admitted.

"Are you both okay?" he asked.

"We are now," I said. "I'm just so sorry."

"You have to believe how sorry *I* am about how I had to lie to you," Mr. McCurdy said.

"No need to lie anymore," Anthony said. "I started to tell them the truth."

"I hated not telling you what was going on and then making up all that stuff about that pretend disease," Mr. McCurdy said.

"We still don't understand why any of this is happening," I said.

Nick grinned. "Yeah, all we know is that Anthony's some sort of cop —"

"Special agent," Anthony corrected from across the room where he was examining Doug's arm. Doug didn't look good.

"Yeah, whatever," Nick said. "And we know there wasn't a disease, but we don't know why you told us there was."

"It was important that you two stay away," Mr. McCurdy said.

"But why didn't you want us here?" I asked.

"It isn't that I didn't want you here — you have no idea how hard it was not to have you two around."

"We have a pretty good idea," I said, "because we know how hard it was not to be here."

"I just didn't have a choice. It's too dangerous for you to be here. It was for your safety."

"We wouldn't get hurt," I said. "We know our way around animals."

"It's not the animals I was worried about," Mr. McCurdy said. "It's all those men who want to buy our animals ... to kill our animals."

"But why are those men coming here?" Nick asked. "And if Anthony's a cop — okay, a special agent — why isn't he arresting them?"

"You can't arrest people without evidence," Anthony said. "But first things first. Bob, you have to take Doug to the hospital to have that arm looked at."

"How bad is it?" Mr. McCurdy asked.

"Collarbone's broken, and I think the arm's fractured," Anthony said.

"I'm so sorry," I said. I felt so awful. I liked Doug. Too bad it wasn't Anthony the elephant had tossed.

"You have nothing to be sorry for," Anthony said. "It isn't like you're the one who tossed him across the barn."

"But if we hadn't have been here, none of this would have happened."

"I guess you have a point there," Anthony said. "Maybe it *is* your fault."

Nick shot me an angry look. I had to learn to keep my mouth shut.

"But there'll be enough time to figure that out later," Anthony said. He turned back to Doug and Bob. "You two better get going to the hospital."

"I don't want to go right now," Doug said. "How about if I wait until tomorrow morning?"

"You go now. You don't have any choice. That's an *order.*"

"But what if something happens tonight and I'm not here to help?" he asked.

"If something happened tonight, you wouldn't be much help, anyway," Anthony reasoned.

"How about if Bob stays here. I don't want to leave you two men short."

"One or two doesn't matter. I need you both. But it doesn't matter. Not now. It's almost two in the morning. If it was going to happen tonight, Vladimir would have called already."

"Just where is Vladimir?" Nick asked.

"He's out trying to arrange a little business deal with a couple of guys who want to buy all of the tigers," Anthony said. "It's a big deal worth close to three hundred thousand dollars."

"You can't sell the tigers no matter how much you get!" I protested.

"Sarah," Mr. McCurdy said, "we're not selling any tigers for any amount of money. This isn't about selling animals. It's about *catching* people."

"Bad people," Anthony said. "Very bad people, and

I'll explain it all in just a few minutes." He turned to Doug. "Call after the doctor's checked you out. Let me know if I need to get another agent for tomorrow."

Bob and Doug left the room, and I heard the sound of the front door closing after them.

"Well?" Nick said. "You were going to explain everything to us."

Anthony nodded. "As you know, I'm a special agent and my assignment is to try to stop the trade in endangered and exotic animals. Tigers are high on that list."

"Then shouldn't you be in the jungles of India or up in Siberia?" Nick asked.

"We have agents in both those places. But what you may not know is that there are far more tigers here in North America than there are in the wilds of India and Siberia put together."

"I didn't know that," Nick said.

"I did," I said. "There are estimates that there are close to twenty-five thousand tigers spread across this continent."

"That's unbelievable!" Nick said.

"Unbelievable but true," Anthony confirmed. "And the vast majority of those are in the hands of private collectors and private game farms."

"People like Mr. McCurdy and Vladimir," Nick said.

"If it was all people like them, there wouldn't be any worries," Anthony said. "Some are owned by people who think nothing about trading a tiger for a wad of cash, and those are the people we're after. We got word out through the Internet, through our website, through contacts in the exotic animal community that there were tigers and other animals for sale and that the buyer didn't need papers or make promises about what he was going to do with the animal. If he had cash, he could get a tiger or whatever animal he wanted."

"And did it work?"

"Like a charm," Mr. McCurdy said. "So far over thirty people have been caught and charged."

"And just as important," Anthony added, "we were able to follow these people back, like links in a chain, to other people and other animals. Thanks to this operation we've saved more than seventy tigers that were waiting for the right bidder or the right butcher."

"That's amazing!" Nick said.

"It is amazing, but why didn't you tell us what was going on?" I asked.

"I wanted to but I couldn't," Mr. McCurdy said.

"I wouldn't let him," Anthony said. "We couldn't risk the operation."

"But we wouldn't have told anybody, honest!" Nick said.

"I'm sure you wouldn't have deliberately told anybody," Anthony said, "but sometimes, for some people, it's hard to hide a lie."

All three of them looked at me. "Is it my fault that I like telling the truth?"

"We just couldn't risk it," Anthony said. "This is too important. Other than Angus and Vladimir, the only other person we told was the head of the local police department."

"Martin knew?" I asked.

"We never run any operation without the cooperation of the local law-enforcement agencies," Anthony said.

"That probably explains why Martin was so insistent

that we not come over here during the quarantine," I said. "He knew it was fake, right?"

"He knew everything," Anthony said. "We had to come up with some story after the two of you almost stumbled into that deal. We had to make sure the deal wouldn't be jeopardized and that you wouldn't be in harm's way. That's when we came up with the disease angle. Actually, the whole part about the parrots was Mr. McCurdy's idea."

"It was your idea?" I asked Mr. McCurdy.

He shrugged. "I couldn't tell you the truth about why you couldn't come out to Tiger Town for a while, so I figured I'd at least tell you a lie that would save your feelings."

"You didn't really think you could fool Sarah for long, did you?" Nick asked.

"I only needed another two or three weeks," Mr. McCurdy said.

"I was surprised it took *this* long," Anthony said.

"Anthony said he thought you'd figure it out, that it was just a matter of time," Mr. McCurdy explained.

"You were suspicious of me from the beginning," Anthony said, "so I thought you'd end up putting two and two together. I figured your bad feelings toward me — the way you don't trust me — would push you in the direction of the truth." He paused, and his trademark smirk slid onto his face. "I bet over the weeks you really started to dislike me."

"I *never* liked you."

Mr. McCurdy cackled like an old crow.

"Didn't you like me even a little in the beginning?" Anthony asked.

I shook my head. "You started with a lie and you always looked like you were hiding something. And what was with those boots?"

"These boots," he said, gesturing at his feet, "were part of a shipment of illegal caiman skins our agents intercepted. I thought they were a perfect touch for the costume of the character I was playing. If you didn't like me to begin with, you must have really, really learned to hate me over the weeks."

"It didn't take that long," I said, and Mr. McCurdy burst into laughter again.

"It was all part of who I had to become to sell this sting operation," Anthony said. "Slimy people like to deal with other slimy people so that's what I became. You have to admit I played it pretty well."

"No argument there," I said.

"You remember when I said the two of us have a lot in common?" Anthony asked.

"I remember," I said, though that didn't mean I agreed.

"Well, we also have one great big difference. We couldn't risk telling you the truth because we couldn't count on you to be able to cover it up. We lied to protect you and your brother."

"But now we know the truth," I said.

"And now it's almost over. Word has gotten out to the exotic animal underground that this is a law-enforcement undercover operation, a sting."

"But you said Vladimir was out meeting with somebody tonight," I said.

"He is," Anthony said. "It's probably our last deal."

"I thought everybody knew about what was really

going on here," I said.

"Everybody in the underground knows, but these people aren't in the underground," Anthony said. "Maybe I shouldn't say any more."

"That's not fair!" Nick protested. "You've told us just about everything already. Besides, who are we going to tell?"

"Go ahead, tell 'em," Mr. McCurdy said.

Anthony sighed. "Okay. There are people in the legitimate animal community, people who run big zoos who aren't much different than these other people. They're prepared to bend or break rules if it means getting the right animal for their zoo. Maybe they want to display them instead of slaughter them, but they're still prepared to buy an animal, no questions asked, that was taken from the wild. Do you know what animal would be the most difficult to acquire?"

"A panda?" I asked.

"A panda would be *impossible* to get," Anthony said, "but you're right. I'm talking about a mountain gorilla."

"A gorilla?" I said. "You have a gorilla here?"

"No, but we don't need to have one as long as people think we have one. If things go right, we're going to sell a gorilla we don't have and in the process catch some people doing things that are illegal."

"Is that why the cameras are in the lights?" Nick asked.

Anthony nodded. "Although they're not just in the lights. There are lots of cameras around the barn and in here." He motioned around the room.

"In here?" I echoed.

"This is where we did a lot of the deals," Anthony

said, "so we needed to record here. And it's not just cameras but microphones. Doug worked the control room, recording all the illegal sales. It makes it hard for somebody to claim they're innocent once they've seen the recordings."

"That's ... that's ... ingenious," I said.

Anthony smiled — not a smirk but a real smile. "Thank you. And now that you know the truth it's important you don't tell anybody, including your mother, what's happening, and that you don't come back here again for at least a few days. Can you both promise that?"

"We can do that," I said.

"Sure," Nick said.

Then the phone rang, and I jumped slightly out of my seat.

"Doug couldn't have been seen already," Anthony said. "They couldn't even be at the hospital yet."

The phone rang again.

"It's not Doug," I said. I knew who it was. "It's our mother."

"We're dead," Nick said.

"Not if we tell her why we were here and ... we can't tell her anything, can we?" I said.

Anthony shook his head. "Sorry. As soon as it's over, you can tell her."

"In that case, you don't have to worry about us coming back because we're going to be grounded until it's over and we can tell her," Nick said.

The phone rang again. "You better get it," I said to Mr. McCurdy. "She's angry, but it'll be worse if she gets more worried."

Mr. McCurdy picked up the phone. "Yep, they're right … Vladimir."

It was Vladimir!

"They want to come now," Mr. McCurdy said.

"They can't come now," Anthony said. "We don't have Doug or Bob here. Tell him we have to delay until tomorrow."

Mr. McCurdy relayed the message and waited for a reply. He lowered the phone from his mouth. "Vladimir says it's now or never. They're really nervous. Either we do the deal right now, they come out to the farm tonight, or they're walking away."

Anthony grimaced, then said, "Tell them … tell them … to come."

Chapter 17

"You two have to go home right now," Anthony said. "They're going to be here in less than an hour."

"But what are you going to do without Bob and Doug?" I asked.

"I'm going to make the deal, talk to those people, and close the deal for the gorilla," Anthony said. He turned to Angus. "And I need you to work the controls in the booth and record the deal."

"Me?" Angus said. "I can't even work my answering machine."

"I could do it," Nick said.

"You?" Anthony asked.

"I've worked the cameras before. I know how to zoom them in and switch from camera to camera. I just don't know about the sound part."

"That's easy," Anthony said. "I could teach you that in a few minutes."

"Nope!" Mr. McCurdy said. "Nick, you have to go home. Both of you have to go home."

"But this guy isn't like the others," Nick said. "You

told us he was from a real zoo. He isn't going to be carrying a weapon, is he?"

Anthony thought for a moment, then said, "He probably won't be."

"And, anyway, I'm going to be far away," Nick said. "I'm going to be in the control room. I can lock the door. It's got to be the safest place in Tiger Town."

"It is safe," Anthony said. "And we really, really need this one recorded. This guy, this zoo director, will be harder to convict if it's just my word against his, because he's a respected member of the community."

"I can do it," Nick said. He turned to Mr. McCurdy. "I can."

"Well ... if you promise you'll stay right in that room and don't come out."

"Fantastic!" Nick crowed.

"If he's staying, then there's no way I'm going anywhere without him," I said.

"I didn't expect you to," Mr. McCurdy said.

"Besides," Anthony said, "if Nick's going to take Doug's place, maybe Sarah can take Bob's."

"What was he supposed to do?" I asked.

"I don't know about Sarah doing that," Mr. McCurdy said, ignoring my question.

"She'll be safe," Anthony said.

"What was he supposed to do?" I asked again.

"She'll be locked in just as tight as Nick," Anthony said. "She'll be just as safe. She will be."

Mr. McCurdy nodded. "I guess she will be locked in."

"Locked in where?" I asked. "What do you want me to do?"

"This deal involves a gorilla," Anthony said. "And they're going to want to see that gorilla."

"But you don't have a gorilla," I said.

"You're right, but we do have this." Anthony walked across the room and picked up a green garbage bag. He opened it and pulled out a fur coat.

What good was a fur coat? I wondered. He reached into the bag again and pulled out a hat — no, it wasn't a hat — it was the head of a monkey. It was a monkey *costume* … a gorilla costume!

"Bob was going to wear this," Anthony said.

"He was going to wear a gorilla costume?" I said. "You can't believe that would fool them into thinking he was a real gorilla, do you?"

"It might if they're not too close and there isn't too much light and the person in the gorilla costume is sitting in a cage behind bars."

"With the door all locked," Mr. McCurdy added.

"And you want me to be in the gorilla costume?"

Anthony nodded.

"You can't be serious."

Nick started to snicker.

"You don't have to if you don't want to," Mr. McCurdy said.

"But it would certainly help us … and help animals," Anthony said.

"Come on, Sarah, do it," Nick said.

I looked at Nick, then at Anthony, and then at Mr. McCurdy. Finally, I nodded and muttered, "I can't believe I'm going to do this."

As quickly as I could, I climbed into the gorilla suit.

"Now put on the head," Nick said.

"I'm already too hot in this monkey outfit, so I'm not putting on the head until I really, really need to."

"Couldn't you put it on for just a few seconds?" Nick asked.

"Why are you so anxious to see me with the head on?"

"It's not for me … it's for Calvin … and for you. I figure if he liked you before, then he's going to *really* like you once he gets a look at you in that suit. This could be love at first sight."

I shook my head, then wondered what time it was. Instinctively, I looked at my wrist. Instead of my watch, though, all I could see was the fur of my gorilla costume.

"Okay, people, it's time to get into position," Anthony said.

"I'm as good as there," Nick said. "This is going to be so cool."

"Just do what I showed you," Anthony said. "And remember, Nick, we're counting on you."

"No problem." Nick started away, stopped, then spun around. "Sarah, be careful."

"You, too," I said as Nick disappeared out the door.

"Time for you to get to your position, as well," Anthony said to me.

"You mean …?"

"In the cage. That's where we keep our gorillas."

He opened the door to the pen. Slowly, I walked over, hesitated for a moment at the entrance, took a deep breath, dipped my head slightly, and entered. There, that wasn't so bad. I'd just find a place to sit and — the door slammed shut behind me and I leaped into the air.

Anthony was now putting a chain in place to seal me in.

"Do you really have to lock it?" I asked.

"If they don't see a lock, they'll know something's wrong. Besides, this way you're safely sealed inside where nobody can get at you ... or examine you too closely."

He wrapped the chain around the bars and then slipped a padlock between two of the links and clicked it shut. I really, really, didn't like this at all.

"Stay in the back corner in the shadows as much as possible," Anthony said. "And if they come over, try to hide your head with one of your arms."

I nodded.

"Put the head on."

"Now?"

"They could be here any time. We have to be ready."

I pulled the head of the costume onto my head and adjusted it so that my eyes were looking out the eyeholes.

"There's a little bit of flap showing on this side," Anthony said. "Tuck it in."

I reached up, fumbled with the place where the head met the rest of the suit, and tucked in a piece of fabric that was sticking out.

"That's perfect."

"Do I really look like a gorilla?"

"As close as we're going to get. There's still one more thing I can do to help disguise the illusion."

Anthony reached up to the light above his head. When he twisted the fluorescent tube, it went out. He walked over to another tube, and then another, until the entire stable area became dingy and bathed in shadows.

"*Now* you look like a gorilla," Anthony said.

I was about to answer when I heard the sound of gravel against tires — they were here!

"Angus and I'll go up and meet them. You stay right here … don't be going anywhere," Anthony said, flashing me one of those smirks.

Mr. McCurdy chuckled. "You make a lovely gorilla, Sarah. Sit tight."

They disappeared out the door, leaving me alone in the semi-darkness, in the barn, in a cage, in the middle of the night … in a gorilla costume. This could be the first time in the entire history of the world that all of those things came together in one place. Just think, right now I could be home in my bed, safe and sound asleep. I shuffled over to the front of the cage and gave the bars of the door a shake. It rattled, but it didn't open. I knew it was locked. I just had to check. Then I heard voices — Vladimir's for sure — and rushed over to the back corner of the cage, where I slumped to the floor.

Vladimir entered the barn along with Mr. McCurdy. Behind them came a man, then a second and a third. Anthony came in last. They walked over and stood in front of the cage — *my* cage. I peeked out at them over top of my arm. The first stranger was in a grey business suit. The second man wore a blue suit. The third newcomer was different. He sported a scruffy leather jacket and jeans and was bigger than the other two. In fact, he was almost as large as Vladimir. And while the others stood right in front of the cage, he lingered off to the side. Instead of looking at me, he kept his eyes on Vladimir, Mr. McCurdy, and Anthony.

"So what do you think of our gorilla?" Mr. McCurdy asked, gesturing toward me.

"Looks small," Grey Suit said.

"It's only a year and a half old, like Vladimir told you," Mr. McCurdy said.

"It looks a bit thin," Blue Suit said. "Is it healthy?"

"He's in good shape," Anthony said. "Good appetite, good activity level."

"It doesn't look too active to me," Grey Suit said. "It's just sitting there."

For a moment I thought about getting up, but I knew my movements would give me away. There was no way I could move like a gorilla. Instead I scratched myself.

"It would be easier if there was more light in here," Grey Suit said.

"It wasn't our idea for you to come in the middle of the night," Mr. McCurdy said. "If you want, you can come back tomorrow. But make it sometime in the afternoon so I can make up for the sleep you cost me tonight."

"No, that's all right," Grey Suit said. "We're here to do business."

"Did you bring the money?" Anthony asked.

The man in the blue suit held up the briefcase he was carrying.

"And it's all there?" Anthony asked. "All eighty-five thousand dollars?"

"All of it," Grey Suit said.

"In the form we requested?" Anthony asked.

"No bills larger than twenties, all old bills, just the way you said it would have to be," Grey Suit confirmed.

"You also realize we're not about to issue a receipt for this money," Anthony said.

The two men in suits chuckled. "We understand the nature of this transaction," Grey Suit said.

"Good. You get your gorilla and we get our money. We're not asking you where you got the money from and you can't be asking us where we got the gorilla. Agreed?"

"That's the agreement," Grey Suit said. "Now we need to examine the gorilla."

Examine? What did he mean by that?

"You can examine all you want as long as you stay on this side of the bars," Mr. McCurdy said.

Grey Suit indicated the man with the briefcase. "I brought my veterinarian along to do a full examination."

"This is a gorilla, not a puppy," Mr. McCurdy said. "You go in there and it'll rip one of your arms off and stuff it up your nose."

"Not if we tranquilize it," Blue Suit said. "Along with the money I have a tranquilizer gun in my —"

"Nobody was supposed to bring any sort of weapons!" Anthony snapped. "As far as I'm concerned, this whole deal is off!"

"No, no, please, we really want to make this deal," Grey Suit pleaded. "Honest!"

Anthony frowned. "Well, I guess we could still go ahead. It was probably just a misunderstanding."

"Exactly," Grey Suit said. "Besides, I hope this will be the first of many deals."

Anthony smiled. "We can supply almost any animal you want. As long as you have the money and realize we're getting the animals through illegal means in violation of international law."

"I don't care where or how you get them as long as you can get them," Grey Suit said.

"Then I think this could be the start of a very long and profitable relationship." Anthony thrust out his hand, and the man in the grey suit moved forward to shake it.

"Sarah! Nicholas! Mr. McCurdy!" It was my mother! She rushed into the stable. Then she saw Mr. McCurdy. "Mr. McCurdy, Sarah and Nicholas are gone and I was hoping —"

"Freeze!" It was the third man. He was holding a pistol!

"All of you, back off!" he yelled.

Nobody moved. It was as if they couldn't believe what was happening.

"Now!" he shouted.

Anthony and Mr. McCurdy hustled over to my mother's side. She looked scared, confused … sleepy.

"What's this all about?" Grey Suit demanded.

"She works for me," Anthony said. "She didn't know what was happening here, but it's okay. She won't talk. Put away the gun before somebody gets hurt."

"You work for him?" the man in the leather jacket asked, pointing the gun at my mother.

"Um … yes … yes, I do."

"And who were you calling for?" he demanded. "Who were you looking for?"

"Sarah and Nicholas," she said.

"Those are her pet *cats*," Anthony said. "She's just looking for her cats."

Even in the dim light I could see the confusion on my mother's face, an expression I was sure the strangers could spot, as well.

"This isn't the way this was supposed to go," Grey Suit said. "But we're going to conclude our business, anyway."

"That's good," Anthony said.

"But with one difference," Grey Suit said. "We're going to keep the money and take the gorilla."

"You can't do that!" Mr. McCurdy said.

"Yes, we can," Grey Suit said. "We have the gun, so we can do what we want. Besides, what are you going to do, call the police and report you were trading in illegal animals? Now give me the keys to the cage."

Nobody moved.

"You have to realize I'm a reasonable person," Grey Suit said, "but my friend with the gun isn't so reasonable. Now give us the keys!"

"You don't want that gorilla," Anthony said. "It's not well. You bring it back to your zoo and you could infect your whole primate program."

"Let me worry about that," Grey Suit said. "We'll tranquilize, examine, test, and quarantine this gorilla to make sure it's not going to cause any troubles. But none of that's your concern. The keys," he said, holding out his hand.

They were going to shoot me with a tranquilizer gun! That couldn't be good!

All three strangers stood with their backs to me, facing Mr. McCurdy, Vladimir, Anthony, and my mother. The man in the leather jacket had his gun trained on them. Somebody had to do something. Maybe I was the somebody.

The strangers' backs almost touched the bars of the cage. Their eyes were focused forward, away from me. Quietly, slowly, I started to crawl toward them. As I moved, the head of my costume shifted to the side so that I couldn't see out of the eyeholes. I reached up and readjusted it so I could see. Then I began crawling again as Grey Suit turned toward me.

"Wait!" Anthony yelled, and Grey Suit pivoted back to look at him.

Obviously, Anthony had seen me move and had also noticed Grey Suit was about to turn and spot me.

"Before you do *anything* hasty," Anthony said, "I need you to *think* about what you're about to do. Think before you *act*!"

This was great! Anthony was going to keep talking and distract them. I came up right behind the strangers.

"Just think," Anthony said. "Sometimes it's best just to *wait*. Anytime there's a gun involved people can get *hurt*, can get *killed*!"

"No one's going to get hurt as long as you all do as you're told," the man with the pistol said.

We'd soon see who was going to tell who what to do. I thrust my hands through the bars and grabbed the arm of the man holding the gun. He shrieked and jumped, pulling me forward and slamming me face first into the bars. I held on tightly as he shook and then spun around, aiming the pistol right at me! There was a thunderous explosion and a brilliant flash of light as I tumbled backwards. The gun was in my hands!

A stampede of bodies followed as Vladimir, Anthony, and Mr. McCurdy rushed forward. The six men started fighting, and my mother began screaming.

I leaped to my feet. "Hold it right there!" I screamed, holding the gun in front of me as if I were in a cop movie.

Nobody stopped. Nobody had even heard me. I aimed the pistol at the floor. I'd never fired a gun before. I'd never even *held* a weapon before. I squeezed the trigger, and the gun jumped as the bullet shot into the floorboards. All at once everybody froze.

"That's better!" I shouted, holding the pistol in front of me but making sure it wasn't actually aimed at anybody. "Now, you three, get up against the wall — now!" I ordered, and they backed up.

"Here, Sarah, you better give me the gun before somebody gets hurt," Anthony said.

I went to hand him the pistol, then stopped. "Nobody gets anything until I get out of this cage and out of this costume."

Anthony smirked, then smiled, and finally saluted.

Chapter 18

"You're going to love this headline!" Nick said as he handed me the evening newspaper.

There, in big letters that filled the entire top of the front page, was: GORILLA GETS GANG! Underneath was a picture of me, still in the monkey suit, holding the head under my arm. The reporter had arrived just after Martin and the rest of the police officers — he'd been listening in on the police band radio and had almost beaten them to the scene of the crime. The story described the arrest of the three men and gave all the details about the others who had been apprehended earlier and the animals the sting operation had saved. The article made it sound as if I was some kind of hero. All I really was, however, was the idiot in the gorilla suit who had forgotten my brother was watching us on the monitors in the control room.

In all of the excitement and with all of the adrenaline coursing through me, I'd forgotten that Nick was there, watching and listening, and as soon as things had gone wrong he had called the police. That was what Anthony had been trying to say to me. He hadn't just been attempting to distract the criminals but had been warning me to *think* and *wait.* I hadn't understood him, though.

It was just luck that the bullet that was fired when I snatched the gun hadn't hit anybody. Thinking back — and now after a good night's sleep I actually was thinking — that was without a doubt the stupidest thing I'd ever done in my whole life. And now, thanks to Nick and those cameras, the whole world had watched it. The morning news had shown the recording twice — once in slow motion. It was eerie seeing just how close my head had been to the gun when it discharged.

Mr. McCurdy walked into the farmhouse kitchen along with Calvin. The chimp raced over and threw his arms around me, giving me a bone-crunching hug. Then, before he even had a chance to think about kissing me, I leaned over and kissed *him* right on the forehead. Calvin threw back his head and howled with laughter, then released his grip.

"I guess a little time in a gorilla suit made you appreciate Calvin more," Mr. McCurdy said.

"I think it's more like a few weeks away from here has made me appreciate everybody more," I said.

"Even me?" Nick asked.

I smiled. "Even you. But most of all I think I appreciate just how much I enjoy being here with everybody and all the animals."

"You don't have to worry about ever being away again," Mr. McCurdy said. "The new changes will make sure of that."

"Changes?" I asked anxiously.

"Maybe I should wait for Anthony to announce it officially," Mr. McCurdy said.

I wasn't sure I'd like anything Anthony would say. I knew in my head he was one of the good guys, but it was still confusing. First he was a bad guy, then a good guy, then a bad guy, and now he was a good guy again.

"I have a question," I said to Mr. McCurdy.

"Yes?"

"One of the reasons we came here was because Kanga and Roo weren't in their pen. Why did you move them into the barn?"

"I wanted to make sure they were safe. I know how much those two little joeys mean to you and, what with all those bad people coming around, I wanted them out of harm's way."

That made sense. I heard the front door open, followed by footsteps, then Anthony appeared in the kitchen. But it wasn't the Anthony I knew. His hair was short again, and he was in clean jeans and a T-shirt. Gone were the cowboy hat and awful caiman boots, the latter replaced by a pair of running shoes. The evil-looking goatee was gone, too.

"You look so different," I gasped.

"I feel so different. It's good to be back wearing my own clothes, being myself again, after dressing and acting like a scumbag. You know I was just acting, right?"

"Of course," I blurted out.

"You even helped me shape the character and the costume," Anthony said.

"I did?"

"I kept watching how you reacted. When I did, said, or wore something you hated, I knew I was on the right track."

"But I never said anything."

"I wasn't listening to your words, but watching your reactions. You really can't hide anything."

"Glad I could help." I wanted to change the subject. "Mr. McCurdy said you were going to tell us about something, some sort of announcement."

"A big announcement. I was going to wait for a press conference to make the formal statement, but there's no harm in you and your brother knowing now. We don't need to keep secrets anymore." Anthony paused. Maybe he'd changed costumes, but he still retained that sense of drama. "Angus has signed papers giving Tiger Town to the Wildlife Conservation Foundation."

"He did what?" I cried. I turned to Mr. McCurdy. "But where will you live?"

"I'll live right here on the farm. Both me and Vladimir."

"They better live here," Anthony said. "As part of the agreement, they'll be employed as the director and executive director of the park — jobs they're free to hold as long as they wish."

"And we're not just getting paid to do the same things we were doing for free," Mr. McCurdy said. "The foundation's going to pay for the continued expansion and operation of Tiger Town."

"More than that," Anthony said, "we're going to try something here that's never been done before. We're going to have a tiger-breeding program, and that program's going to attempt to release those tigers back into the wild."

"That's amazing!" Nick said.

"And Vladimir and me can't wait to get started," Mr. McCurdy said. "Isn't that wonderful, Sarah?"

"Yeah, wonderful … it's just that … just that …"

"That it's never been done before," Anthony said, completing the sentence I didn't want to finish.

I nodded.

"You're right," he agreed. "It's never been done before, but if anybody can do it, I think Angus and Vladimir can."

"We're sure enough going to try," Mr. McCurdy said, "but we're going to need a lot of help."

"You have the full support of the foundation," Anthony said. "We'll provide anything and everything you'll be needing."

"I might still need a little more help," Mr. McCurdy said. He looked directly at my brother and me. "Nick? Sarah?"

"You know you can count on me!" Nick said enthusiastically. "You couldn't keep me away even when you tried!"

"That's my boy!" Mr. McCurdy said. "And you, Sarah?"

I shrugged. "I'll do whatever I can, but I really don't know if I can be much help."

Mr. McCurdy grinned. "Sarah, without you, practically none of the wonderful things that have happened around here would have ever happened. We need you, girl."

"Then I'm in for whatever comes next."